The Top

Julie heaved a dramatic sigh and blew the air out between her pursed lips slowly. "Gee, Kathy, you must really want it so bad it hurts."

"Want what?"

"To *win*. To go to the top. Otherwise you wouldn't put up with all this garbage."

Kathy ripped off a new batch of seaweed. "I never thought of it that way," she said at last. "But you're right, you know. I do want it that bad. I want to be the New England tennis champion this year. I'd run to the North Pole barefoot if it meant I'd win. Stupid, of course, because I don't have a hope this year. But it's almost like a taste in my mouth. It's like when your mouth is parched and you see a big glass of water and you can just taste it."

When No One Was Looking

ROSEMARY WELLS

SCHOLASTIC INC.
New York Toronto London Auckland Sydney

ISBN 0-590-43514-0

12 11 10 9 8 7 6 5 4 3 2 1   1 2 3 4 5 6/9

Printed in the U.S.A.   01

First Scholastic printing, March 1991

To Tom

Because Julia was beautiful and had a classic forehead, Miss Greco had chosen her to model for one of her many ceramic heads. Wildly differing students had posed for Miss Greco over the years, but the heads looked remarkably alike. In the back of the classroom Kathy Bardy waited for Julia. The questions in her algebra book lay horribly unsolved before her. Kathy fidgeted over them and dreamed in the sweet June air, looking for some sign of Julia's features in Miss Greco's brick-colored Plastilina. As yet there was none. The heads on the windowsill resembled not only one another but the work of Miss Greco's favorite sculptor, whose lumpy, suffering peasants, published in *Art News*, decorated the bulletin board. There was an air of humility about Miss

Greco that Kathy found unsettling. It seemed that Miss
Greco was cheerfully resigned to being a high school art
teacher who struggled to imitate the private style of a
famous man. She appeared to accept without regret
her mousy thinning hair and her dust-coated ortho-
pedic shoes, which tracked up even the ladies' room
floor, and Kathy, had she wakened one morning to find
herself in Miss Greco's place, would have certainly
jumped out a window.

"No, you wouldn't," said Julia later on the way to the
club.

"A high window," Kathy added.

In a southern voice that purred as agreeably as the
engine of her silver Mercedes 6.9, Mrs. Irene Beaufort
Redmond, Julia's mother, declared that suicide was an
unseemly topic of conversation. "My Kathy," which was
what she always called her daughter's best friend, "will
never jump out any window on God's green earth, because she is number one."

"Number twelve," Kathy amended.

"Number one, number twelve, it's all tacky business
anyway," said Julia's mother.

Kathy knew that was true in a sense; however, she did
not like her ranking taken frivolously. Mrs. Redmond
continued, "And my Julia is also a number one, but I
wish, darling, you would take up some challenge like
your friend Kathy has taken up tennis. Life has been too
easy for you this far, and you need a challenge."

Julia met this suggestion with silence and a wink at
Kathy. Tennis, after all, was not something that Kathy
had *taken up*, as a person might take up reading the

horoscopes in the paper. At the time, over a year ago, when tennis had more or less happened to Kathy, she'd still harbored dreams of becoming the first woman short-stop for the Boston Red Sox.

They had discovered her "talent" one day at a tennis clinic which had been squeezed in between a fireman's parade and the annual VFW Easter-egg hunt. The tennis people all talked about talent, and now even Kathy's parents used the word, as if she were some sort of rising Rembrandt.

There was no denying that this was exciting. Kathy's family had "no money," as her mother put it, unlike Julia's family, who had "real money." Kathy had none of her younger sister Jody's brains, or if she did, this did not show in her schoolwork. She did not possess Julia's good looks and easy manner. Tennis had come suddenly to Kathy, like the unexpected winning of a state lottery. And like those gleeful lottery winners pictured in the papers grinning among the signals of poverty that were theirs moments before, Kathy cherished tennis, and out-wardly she reveled in it.

Mrs. Redmond blew kisses through the car window to both "her girls." "I'll come get you at five thirty," she said, "so Kathy has time for a swim after her lesson."

"I'm on lifeguard duty tonight," said Kathy. "It's the first club dance of the season, and someone always winds up in the pool."

"You work too hard, darling," Mrs. Redmond an-swered sadly. "Just don't pull any drunks out of the pool. Drunks are always dead-weightenized." With this statement and ten more kisses Mrs. Redmond and the silver Mercedes glided away down the long petunia-lined pebble drive.

"You do work too hard," said Julia when her mother had gone, for Julia never agreed with her mother if her mother was present. "Maybe when school's out, you'll have some time and we can just do nothing a little, the way we used to. You ought to get a tan, Kath, without the lines from your tennis dress."

Kathy straightened her rackets and took the cover and press off one of them. "I'll be lounging around with an algebra book. That's what," she said.

"Oh, come on. The final won't be that bad. Don't worry. I'll help you. You'll pass."

Kathy grunted at her racket press.

"Why don't you come for a quick Coke? You have time before your lesson," Julia asked in an abnormally cheerful voice.

"Julia, you *know* I have to do the courts."

"I know! I know!" Julia answered, raising a hand and shutting her eyes against this fact. "Give my hate to old Miss Pus-bucket."

"I will," said Kathy, and she walked slowly over to the courts past a series of whitewashed iron urns which had been newly planted with red-and-white-striped petunias. She would have liked to have a Coke and laugh for half an hour or so.

In Kathy's view there were few things Julia did not understand with a quick and visceral reflex. The whole business of being talented was a thing Julia took quite for granted, as she took the fact of having money or having perfect teeth. She accepted Kathy's new-found genius as if, in storybook fashion, Kathy had suddenly inherited a million dollars from a long-lost uncle. Julia welcomed Kathy's still-tender ascendancy in the game of tennis with an I-told-you-all-along outlook that was childlike and grown-up at the same time. On the other hand, Kathy decided, Julia had no grasp of the need for working at anything. Whether Kathy had to work at odd jobs for money or work grueling, sweaty hours in the hot sun or on the public courts at night, Julia viewed hard work as an invention of unimaginative adults who had lost all sense of fun in this world. Having an immense library of first editions at home, many of them read to her aloud years before the school system tackled the same books, and having been to Europe several times, Julia came easily to her A-plus average, as if in every subject she had been already thoroughly educated. Algebra, English, drawing, and riding, all these things were to Julia pleasant diversions, presenting no more difficulty than the eating of an artichoke. Because of this, or perhaps in spite of it, Julia was not popular at school.

Whether this bothered Julia or not anymore, Kathy didn't really know. Mrs. Redmond had always dismissed as hilariously petty anything that happened in school. At the same time Julia's father was subject to occasional seizures of New England prudence and insisted that Julia stay in the public school and ride the school bus just like everybody else.

Kathy recalled vividly the second day of first grade. Behind the massive blue velvet curtain on the gymnasium stage the girls had all undressed to be weighed and measured by the school nurse. Someone had poked fun at Julia's underwear. When Julia pointed out that it had been handmade in France and was much prettier than the nylon underwear of the girl who was picking on her, a crowd had gathered instantly. They jeered so cruelly at Julia's dress, which was also handmade and too conservative in style, and at her diction, which had been carefully groomed by a succession of English nannies, that Julia had sat on the floor and cried miserably. After school that day Kathy had found Julia crouched behind a hedge, afraid to get on the bus and still in tears. Not even knowing Julia's name, Kathy had sat beside her on the school bus and threatened to kill anyone who brought up the subject of underwear or accents again.

From that day on Kathy and Julia had been the best of friends, but Julia had established a pattern and never really pulled herself out of it. She was laughed at for bringing sandwiches of pâté de foie gras to school. Kathy remembered Julia pleading with her mother to give her tuna fish instead. Mrs. Redmond replied by saying that she'd never bought a can of tuna fish in her life and wasn't about to, since the smell would drive a starving dog from the room. Kathy had repressed her hurt at this skewering of her own mother's lunches because she was totally in awe of everything Mrs. Redmond did or said. Julia was laughed at because sometimes her grandmother picked her up from school in a chauffeur-driven car and because she missed classes with abandon for family vacations. Later she was teased for having a perfect accent in French.

Private school had been discussed from time to time, but since this would have required Julia to get up at seven in the morning instead of eight, Julia had out-right balked and once had spent three days with a large piece of masking tape over her mouth, refusing to eat or drink until her mother dropped the subject. Whereas Kathy's nature tended toward violent physical self-defense, jealousy, and blurting out whatever was on her mind at the moment, Julia avoided all conflicts. She waded through whatever souls dared to tease her like a missionary doctor among the lepers, completely un-afraid of catching leprosy. This attitude worked wonders as it tended to drive a tormentor to ridiculous extremes. Julia knew she was envied more than hated, and so she had a sunny nature, and she and Kathy had spent the last eight years laughing at practically everything.

The petunias in the decorative urns had five stripes apiece, Kathy noticed, except for the few that had six. This only reminded her of the algebra final to come. Kathy pictured the final as if it were a huge bloated dead fish on the horizon, and she felt a wrench of jealousy toward Julia and the ease with which Julia faced such things as exams. She could no more rid herself of the jealousy than she could wish away her anger when she found herself losing a tennis match. Julia, Kathy reminded herself, had never been jealous of any-thing or anyone so far as Kathy knew, with the brief exception of Laura Mae Bullock, who had stolen Robbie Martin, Julia's first real crush, away from her. Since Laura Mae had terrible acne and a reputation for doing things with boys behind the town water tower, Julia had not been jealous long. She had welcomed Kathy's success at tennis with astonishing openheartedness, even though it took Kathy away from her company for long hours. Of course there was a reason for this. Kathy's many tournaments, trophies, free rackets from Spalding, and her interview in the *Herald American* cut right through all the uncomfortable class and money business that was the only thing that had separated them since the first grade. It legitimized, like a new moon wish come true, a rite of eternal friendship both girls had performed, using the blood of a dead pigeon, when they were six and a half. It somehow made all right those times that their fathers, on meeting now and then in the Sears tool department or while buying the Sunday papers, had nodded and grunted to each other in recognition of their daughters but had said little more. Now Julia's father would say hello and ask after Kathy's latest victory, and her father would grin and fold up the sports pages and be wonderfully modest about the whole thing. Carefully Kathy hid her new sense of equality from Julia. From time to time she would mention Evert's backhand or Andrea Jaeger's nerve but never the prize money she read about with such awe. Unlike death, religion, and the details of menstruation, neither Kathy nor Julia ever alluded to money.

Kathy supposed that come Tuesday, Julia, ever-generous, would slide her paper and move her arm during Mrs. Diggins's abominable final algebra exam and that she, Kathy, would find it too great a temptation.

"Where is your mind, my dear?" asked Marty in Kathy's imagination. Kathy checked to see whether Marty was in her office. She was, as she always was at two thirty on Fridays, counting the week's take. Kathy could see her silhouette, feet on the desk, Coke bottle in hand in the little white clapboard building, salt-licked and surrounded by more petunias in the window boxes. Kathy would not go in, as Marty disliked being interrupted while she was counting money. Half an hour remained before her lesson would begin, and in order to pay part of her membership fee for the Plymouth Bath and Tennis Club, Kathy had to pick up all the balls from the morning's lessons and sweep the first three courts clean. Brushing the soft green dust from the tapes and collecting balls from the thistles and shells outside the fence gave Kathy time to play with her thoughts. She didn't mind the work at all, except she knew Marty was watching every move she made. Marty always did that, because Kathy Bardy was her pet.

Contemptuous of most of her summer pupils' indifferent efforts to achieve a clean forehand, Marty had a string of nicknames for them. She called the most private of their weaknesses to their attention, knowing they would never admit to their parents to being called Jelly-rump or Pig-eyes. Marty was not well liked. It was said of her that had she been a swimming coach instead of a tennis coach, she would have tossed a baby off the jetty in January and expected it to swim to shore. But because Marty had suffered third degree burns over every inch of her body as a child and had been given up for a lifelong cripple, only to recover and beat Maureen Connolly at Wimbledon, thereby causing her name to be emblazoned on a line of Wilson rackets, Marty was somehow forgiven.

There were things said, and things left unsaid. One of the things that was said most often of Kathy was that she had a phenomenal gift, was the most promising New England girl to come along in ages. It was said that she would go "right to the top" if she learned to control her temper.

It was said that Marty was the only first-class woman coach in the country. (Proven most recently by Kathy's jump from unknown to twelfth in New England in her age category and fourth in the district in the space of fourteen months.)

It was not said that Marty, whose days of glory came when tennis had been a gentlewoman's game and therefore unpaid, had a great stake in Kathy Bardy's future or that she had her eye on the prodigies and the publicity that would be hers should Kathy turn professional and become famous like Tracy Austin. Kathy was half-aware of the connection between her future and Marty's.

It was not said that Kathy's father worried about the money all this cost. Kathy was very aware of this, not in terms of sums or exact figures but in the same simple way that she knew by looking out the window whether it was raining.

It was not said (even by Kathy to herself) that at this very moment, when she ought to have been mentally preparing herself for tomorrow's tournament in Quincy, she was instead avenging Carl Yastrzemski's pop-up in the playoffs against the hated Yankees.

At exactly three o'clock Marty tossed her Coke bottle into the trash barrel and sauntered out onto the court. Her face, mildly scarred under a brilliant red head of hair, looked always to Kathy like the face of the joker in a deck of cards. Every day Marty wore an identical tennis outfit, a white dress, unfashionably long. It matched the dress in the photo that hung in her office of that day long ago when she'd been victor over the famous Maureen. Kathy wondered for the hundredth time why Marty clung to such things as the dress and, biting clean as they were, the old-fashioned high wool socks and old-fashioned deck sneakers instead of wearing Adidas or Tretorns. Marty scoffed at all changes. She would not tolerate metal rackets or a two-handed backhand no matter what Chris Evert had done. She also frowned on all the money the pros made. Officially Marty insisted that tennis was a ballet, a game of joy and a sport worthy of angels, and that the flashing about of six-figure incomes was ruinous to its spirit. However, she possessed a memory like a tax collector for every penny the pros turned over, and she repeated these statistics from time to time in between commands to "Keep the head *down*" and "Move, dammit, move!"

"Where is your mind, my dear?" Marty asked. "My dear" was her nickname for Kathy.

Kathy reddened. She had hit three backhands in a row directly at Marty instead of down the line. "I'm sorry, Marty."

"I want you to play like a man, not like a lady who paints teacups on the side. Is that clear?"

"Yes, Marty."

"You'll never be any good unless you learn to play like a man. How do you think Althea Gibson got where she got?"

Kathy searched her memory for the name Althea Gibson. Out of what attic did Marty drag these names? "She played like a man," said Kathy, who knew how to answer a question.

"She served like a man, she rushed the net like a man, and she was over six feet tall. You, my dear, are a shrimp and so have twice as far to go." Marty's logic was as wicked as her ability to return shots from mid-court. For an hour Kathy hit the same backhand shot down the same line.

"Why are you smiling?"

"I'm not smiling," said Kathy, smiling.

"Are you smiling because you think you're going to have such an easy time with Alicia deLong over the weekend? Alicia is number five."

"No," Kathy answered, this time not smiling.

"Are you smiling because you think you've done so well? That's for me to tell you, isn't it?"

"Yes, Marty."

"Well then, why are you smiling? Put on your sweater. Answer me."

Kathy was too frightened to remember what had brought a smile to her face, "Just something . . ." she began, "at school."

"Where is your mind, my dear?" Marty asked again, bending over for a ball. "After next week there'll be no school to distract you. Now what are you crying for?"

Kathy sat down on the spectator's bench in the shade of a green-and-white-striped awning. She tried to concentrate on a girl serving endlessly on court six.

"Why are you crying?"

"I'm not . . . anymore."

"Do you have your period?"

"No. That never bothers me anyway."

"Don't be a fool, of course it bothers you. I keep track of you. I know. Stop looking embarrassed. You know you never remember when you're going to get it."

Kathy sat silent, not because this was the thing that Marty could least stand but because nothing safe to say occurred to her. This was like an algebra test at its worst, like Chinese or Greek. "I may have to take tutoring this summer," she managed to squeak out at last. Perhaps Marty would turn her wrath in another direction.

"In what? Tutoring for what?"

"Algebra. I can't possibly pass the final."

"Algebra! Why? Fail! Who cares? You think the USTA cares about algebra?"

"My folks do, especially my father," said Kathy.

"I have told your parents a hundred times that you shouldn't be pushed in all directions at once. The kind of pressure you're under now doesn't allow for algebra," said Marty bitterly.

"My teachers say the opposite, you know. If I don't improve my schoolwork next year, I'm sure they'll never let me go at one thirty to practice every day in Swampscott."

Marty chewed on her lower lip and then, amazingly, she whispered "Kathy" quite gently and covered Kathy's hand with her own. "Don't cry," she began in what Kathy knew was a voice that did not come easily to her. "Just think, one day all this schoolwork will be over. You'll just have your game to think about, and you're going to be right on the top. In the Wightman Cup, at Wimbledon. No one is going to touch you, not even the little rich girls with twenty years of tennis clubs behind them. You're going to show them all. But remember, your family isn't rich. You don't have the advantages some girls have. You'll never be much of a student. This is the one way you're going to break out of all the dullness in life. You're going to go to England and France someday, Kathy. You'll go to Rome and win the Italian championship. Think of that! And everyone who says a New Englander can't do it, a girl who takes up tennis late can't do it, a girl with a woman coach can't do it— well, they're all going to be eating crow someday. That algebra teacher of yours is going to sit back in her Jordan Marsh rocker and *read* about you in the papers someday, and maybe you'll give her an autograph. I've been there, Kathy. I held up that silver plate in front of the Queen of England, and I know."

Kathy knew two things. One was that Marty wouldn't be likely to put her hand on her own mother's if her mother had been run over by a car. The other was that Marty was being uncanny, as she was when it suited her. The phrase *show them all* had hit Kathy surgically, in the center of her belly. Yes, she wanted to show them all, although she didn't know who "they" were. "Who's that on court six?" Kathy asked at last.

"Nobody," said Marty, withdrawing her hand.

"Just because she's new doesn't make her nobody. She has a strong serve."

Marty sighed. "She's big, she's slow, and she has weasely eyes. She's one of Gordon's brand-new lesser lights."

Gordon was the other coach in this part of New England. Once upon a time he too had been one of Marty's pets, but he hadn't the temperament to go very far. Gordon was handsome and popular and had many promising juniors in his stable. Marty had not spoken to him in years. "Foot fault," said Marty, glaring at the girl. "She has big feet."

"She has a strong serve," repeated Kathy.

"She's as big as a lumberjack."

Kathy picked up her rackets and her bag. "She's got a strong serve, Marty."

"And as clumsy," Marty continued, as if Kathy had said nothing.

Kathy knew it was hopeless to try and get in the last word, so she left Marty, promising to call after the next day's matches. Once she looked back. Marty was concentrating on the girl, sitting alone on the newly painted white bench. Kathy had few moments of true revelation, but she did wonder as she crossed the neatly raked parking lot to join Julia for a swim whether Marty, gnarled and scarred, had such a thing as a mother.

As she mentioned all odd thoughts to Julia, Kathy mentioned this one when she'd come up from the water and settled herself in a deck chair.

"That's a funny thing to say. Everyone has a mother."

"I know. But Marty's old. Past forty or fifty maybe. I thought her mother might have died in that fire when she was a baby."

"Are you trying to excuse her awfulness?" Julia asked.

"No, not that. I just felt sorry for her suddenly."

Julia rolled her eyes heavenward. She imitated her own mother's drawl precisely. "No one on God's green earth I feel sorry for less than that mean, hungry woman." And then, switching to her regular voice, Julia said that not even a childhood spell in a concentration camp would excuse Marty's excesses in her eyes.

"Excesses," repeated Kathy.

"You take more you-know-what from that coach than I can believe. I couldn't. I *couldn't*. I'd cry like a baby or spit in her eye. I don't know which."

Kathy stretched and threw her towel over an empty chair. "You have to get to know her," she said.

"There's something about her that I hate," Julia said slowly. "I don't even really hate my Aunt Liz, who threw a vase at Mom on her last visit, but I hate that Marty."

"Why?" Kathy asked.

Over the top of her magazine Julia looked Kathy in the eye, and without wavering as Kathy would have done she declared, "Because she's mean to you, and I don't like people being mean to you."

For the second time that day Kathy asked in embarrassment, "I wonder who that is?"

"I don't know," said Julia, "but she's a powerful swimmer. Probably races. Look at her strokes."

The same large body that had been serving so steadily in court six now swam up and down the length of the pool with identical determination. She was still at it long after Julia had left and the evening shadows had fallen on the pool, the deck, and the surrounding empty chairs. At last she hoisted herself out and announced to no one, "Two hundred."

By this time Kathy had finished a hamburger and a soda (free to employees of the club) and had started to net a few limp ginko leaves off the surface of the water. She collected what stray wet towels lay around and cleaned out the pool house. The club manager would check her work later with the energy of a room inspector at West Point. She lined up the containers of chlorine, although they were already arranged perfectly. Then she collected the things for the lost-and-found box and took them to the office. The previous summer Kathy had been the lone club employee without a single red stroke beside her name on the manager's error sheet, or blacklist, as it was called by the lifeguards. She enjoyed this little contest, and the work required no thought at all. At seven, when the first people arrived for the dance, the pool house was immaculate, the water leafless and shimmering, and the deck as shiny as a liner's on a maiden voyage. Kathy buttoned her sweater against the wind and climbed high up into her lifeguard's chair. There she sat in the darkness, listening to the ocean wash and spill against the rocky jetty outside the three-story enclosure of lockers and public rooms that left the pool open to the sky, staring into the wonderful depths of the lighted water. She was quite happy. In one hour she would begin passing the rest of the evening listening to the Red Sox on a tiny transistor radio she kept hidden in her towel.

"I'm Oliver English," said a voice from the deck. The voice cracked slightly in the middle of the sentence. "I'm afraid I got you into trouble with your coach."

"Trouble?" Kathy asked. A boy with very heavy glasses and large white teeth was smiling up at her. But of course she remembered right away. He *had* indirectly gotten her into trouble with Marty. It had been Oliver whom she'd seen grinning at her at the end of her lesson, and she of course had smiled back. Marty had probably figured him to be a potentially more serious distraction than algebra.

"She's pretty tough on you. She's a real drill sergeant," Oliver added.

Kathy laughed. "I know," she said, "but she's nicer to me than she is to anyone else. I'm quite used to her."

"I'm the other lifeguard tonight," Oliver announced. "You're the best girl tennis player I've ever seen. Will you hit with me next week? I've played a lot out in California."

"Sure," said Kathy, and she began to laugh.

"Why are you laughing? You think you can beat me?" Oliver looked seriously annoyed behind his horn-rims.

Kathy pointed to the dance, now fully under way in the conservatory, a room reserved for senior members. People had gathered around the bar and talked in little groups, although no one danced yet. A woman in an evening dress, tall as an oak, stood holding a drink in both cupped hands. She was listening to a man in Madras pants. Her smile never wavered from a full horsy grin, and she wore a diamond choker that could be seen twenty yards away. The flashing teeth and sparkling diamonds complemented each other perfectly. "Look at her!" Kathy said. "Look at him! Don't they seem big to you? That guy must weigh three hundred pounds. What would we do if he fell in the pool?"

"That's what *I'm* here for," said Oliver seriously.

"But that's why I'm laughing," said Kathy. "You're not much bigger than I am. It would take four of us to pull him out of an armchair."

"I'm seventeen," said Oliver, glaring at Kathy, "and I'm on the Yale freshman crew."

"You must be strong," said Kathy hurriedly.

"I'm very strong." The corners of Oliver's mouth turned down like the mask of tragedy. He continued to look unhappy behind his glasses, which, as if they came in sizes like shirts, appeared to be a size too big for him. "It isn't a question of weight," he went on. "I could pull a whale out of the pool if I got the right grip on him. It's all in the grip, or didn't they teach you that in life-saving?"

"I guess you're right," Kathy answered. She noticed that Oliver's black hair danced wildly in the wind. He wore it long over the front and very short at the back like World War Two fighter pilots she'd seen in late movies on TV. His skin was as clear and pink as a baby's, his chest as hairless as Kathy's, and although she knew she could have hidden her whole fist in the depression between his ribs, she liked him. "Who's your girl friend?" Oliver asked huffily.

"Girl friend? Oh, Julia. The one I was sitting with."

"She's pretty. Very pretty," said Oliver.

"I know," said Kathy, hoping she didn't betray any jealousy in her voice, and she told herself Julia would never have made a mess out of meeting a boy as she had done.

"Molina!" said Oliver suddenly and poked Kathy's foot. "Look sharp!"

Out of the brilliantly illuminated assortment of drinkers and eaters at the other end of the clubhouse came the Plymouth Bath and Tennis Club manager. Busy as a hornet, he glanced at his clipboard as if he wished he could yell at it. "One of you," he said to Kathy and Oliver, "is supposed to be in one chair, and the other is supposed to be in the other chair." He paused for a tiny breath. "And who, may I ask, selected you two to be lifeguards at an adult party? This is not a toddler swim hour."

"But, Mr. Molina," Kathy began, "I got a letter telling me to work tonight and . . ."

"And you?" Mr. Molina interrupted.

"The same thing, sir," said Oliver.

"That's my secretary's fault, of course," said Mr. Molina. "She doesn't know one from another. We have six big boys much better suited. You couldn't pull a baby out of the shallow end," he observed to Oliver.

"But—" Kathy began.

"It's not your fault!" Mr. Molina shouted. "Now go pick up that towel over there. Have you checked the chlorine level in the pool?"

"Yes," said Kathy.

"One of you pick up that Coke bottle before someone trips over it and winds up in the hospital. I'm going to keep an eye on both of you. No fraternization. You sit in one chair, and he sits in the other. You have a job to do, and you're paid twenty dollars each to do it, so do it." And twittering to himself like a head nurse on duty, Mr.

Molina went back to the clubhouse, looking right and then left and walking in the exact center of the indoor-outdoor carpeting.

In a loud whisper Kathy asked Oliver why he hadn't said anything about it all being in the grip.

"Oh, shut up," said Oliver, also in a loud whisper.

Nobody fell in the pool. Like two undersized sentries, Kathy and Oliver slouched in their widely separated chairs. The drains gurgled from time to time. *Why do they always look at Julia?* Kathy asked herself. *He'll probably sit with her all summer, and I'll be left out like someone's extra little sister. Why do I have to be flat-chested and have dull hair? Why won't Dr. Morrissey take my braces off? If I hit with him next week, he'll want to play a set, and I'll beat him, and he'll never speak to me again. Why everything?* Kathy did not dare put on the Red Sox game.

"Are your folks here?" asked Oliver suddenly.

"No. They're . . . not members," Kathy answered.

"How come?"

Kathy began fabricating her usual reason in her mind, that her mother was allergic to the sun, that her father didn't like the ocean because of a wartime trauma in the Pacific. "They can't afford it," she said.

"They pay for just you to belong?"

"They have to. I'm on lifeguard duty every day I can and work at the courts and in the lunchroom to help. My younger sister, Jody, waits tables in the cafeteria week-ends, and my brother Bobby's just a baby, so he comes free when Jody's off and she can watch him."

"What do you mean, they have to?" Oliver asked.

"This is my tennis coach's summer job, at this club. I have to work with her at least five times a week. The courts are excellent clay, and there're good people to hit with. I have to belong because it's the best thing for my game."

"You mean you're serious about tennis? Are you a ranked player and everything?"

"Yes, I guess so," said Kathy, staring at her toes and wishing the subject would go away.

"Are you going to be a professional?"

"My mom and dad and my coach think I have a chance. First I have to qualify for the National Championships. If I'm lucky enough to get national ranking in my age group, maybe I can take it from there in a few years. I'm number twelve now in fourteen and under, but that's just New England. One in a million makes it to pro."

"I'm still impressed," said Oliver.

"Don't be," said Kathy.

"Do you like it?" he asked.

"Sure I like it. I couldn't spend twenty hours a week practicing if I didn't like it. And my mom has to drive me to tournaments and bring the kids along almost every other weekend. My dad has to pay for court fees and lessons and everything."

"But do you really like it?"

"I want to win the U.S. Open someday," said Kathy, and she surprised herself with the coldness of her own voice.

Oliver folded his hands between his bony knees. "But do you like it?" he asked again.

"Why do you keep asking me that?"

"Because when you said just then that you wanted to win the U.S. Open, you sounded so awful. I didn't really mind you laughing at me before, and you sounded just like a . . . person then, not just a girl. Now you sound like everybody else at this club. Like the stockbrokers who get drunk here on the beach Sunday afternoons."

Kathy could think of no reply to that. Not even Julia addressed her so frankly as this odd boy. "I'm sorry," she murmured after a minute had passed.

"What happens if you don't win the U.S. Open?" Oliver persisted. "Supposing you don't make it that far?"

"I'll have to go to college and just have a normal life, I guess. I'll have to think about my grades too, not just tennis, or I'll never get in anywhere good."

"But what would you like to be more than anything else?"

"I just told you," said Kathy.

"But if you don't make it."

"Well, you'd laugh at me," said Kathy, playing with the life preserver that hung on the side of her chair.

"No, I won't."

"I could never tell a boy," said Kathy.

"What?" asked Oliver heatedly. "A urologist?"

"What's that?" Kathy asked.

"A doctor who operates on men's privates," said Oliver.

"No! Of course not!" Kathy whispered angrily. "What made you think of that of all things?"

"Well," said Oliver, pushing his glasses up his nose, "if you don't win the U.S. Open and you don't want to be a urologist, what do you want to be?"

How did this happen? Kathy asked herself. "Shortstop for the Red Sox," she said weakly. "I played little league until I was about twelve and then I started tennis full time."

"Oh! Well, that's not so bad. I wanted to pitch once. I'm a very good pitcher. I've got a nice slider, but I'm too small to make the Yale team."

Kathy wished she could just tell Oliver how much she liked him for not laughing at her, but instead she pretended to gaze at the dancers. She tapped her foot in time to "Some Enchanted Evening." "It doesn't matter, being small," she said when the music was over. "I'm a shrimp, but I'm still going to beat 'em all."

"There you go again," said Oliver, grinning.

"Who on earth was that?" Kathy's mother asked after Kathy had jumped into the front seat of the station wagon and wrapped a towel around herself for warmth. "Where's your sweater? Who was that boy?"

"I lent him my sweater," said Kathy. "He was cold."

"You lent him your sweater!"

"It's my tennis sweater. It looks okay on a boy."

"Kathy, that's a fifty dollar sweater. Who was that funny looking boy?" Mrs. Bardy ran the fingers of her left hand through her hair, a masculine gesture that Kathy had not inherited and did not like. Her mother did this when she was worried or tired. It occurred to Kathy that her mother seemed worried or tired a great deal of the time. She was always pinching the bridge of her nose under her glasses in weariness. Her mother had never cared for hairdos or clothes or pretty objects, but recently she seemed to care even less for these things. Her time was divided in three parts: work, family, and Kathy's tennis. As for the latter Kathy wished she could relieve her mother in some way, but that of course was impossible. Once upon a time her mother had been an athlete too, with a strong, hard body that looked so healthy and young that she didn't need plucked eyebrows or lovely dresses. Ten years behind the counter at the photo shop had made her pallid and soft, or was it just the contrast with Julia's beautiful mother that Kathy saw? "His name is Oliver English," said Kathy, "and he goes to Yale."

"He looks like an orphan."

"He is an orphan. Well, practically."

"What do you mean, practically?" Her mother's voice was impatient, as she liked everything to be exact.

"Well, he's here for the summer, living with an uncle, I think. His father is somewhere up in the deserted part of Canada, and he can't live with his mother and stepfather because his stepfather hates him, and he hates his stepfather because he gambled away most of his mother's money at the racetrack and playing cards."

"They sound like absolutely awful people. I don't want you mixed up with people like that, Kathy. Gambling, of all things!"

"Oliver isn't awful, Mother. He can't help his stepfather. He even put tacks under his stepfather's tires when he was eleven years old. Besides, Mother, these things happen very frequently. Often stepfathers don't get along with their new wives' sons. The Chinese say the son bites the toe of the stepfather."

"What?" Mrs. Bardy turned and looked at Kathy with something close to horror on her face.

"Oliver's major is Oriental languages, Mother. At Yale. At Yale!"

"Oliver seems to have told you a great deal about himself," said her mother, meaning something entirely different. Kathy, through the drone of the motor and the singing of the cicadas, could almost hear her mother ask, *What did you tell him about us? Did you mention that Grandma is in a nursing home too expensive for us but not expensive enough to be good? Did you say that twenty years ago I did not even come close to making the Olympic swimming team and that I use tea bags twice? Did you tell him Daddy works as a commercial photographer going to other people's weddings and bar mitzvahs and confirmations, or did you try to make Daddy's job sound artistic?* But of course her mother did not ask any of these questions, which was a shame because, although Kathy felt estranged from her family at various times, she would no more have parted with any of this information than she would have described herself going to the bathroom.

"Oliver's sweet, Mother," said Kathy. "He's not like regular dumb boys at all. He isn't all pimply and aggressive. He has no mother and father to take care of him. He doesn't even have a sweater. He has to eat crummy old hamburgers at the club every night because his uncle doesn't get around to shopping. Can we have him to dinner Thursday night?"

"Did you invite him, Katherine? Did you?"

"No," Kathy lied. "I'm hitting with him Thursday

afternoon, though. He's ranked twenty in Boys' Eighteen and Under in California." Another complete lie.

"He is?"

"Yes, and he deserves a decent dinner, I think."

Her mother's tone changed. "We can have him. Yes, Kathy, I think it would be very good for you to hit with a good boy for a change, and I feel sorry for him too. But I want to make one thing absolutely clear."

"Yes, Mother."

"You are too busy with tennis and school to have anything else on your mind right now. You may not start dating and riding around on other people's motorcycles."

"Yes, Mother. And, Mother?"

"What is it?"

"Oliver has a twelve-year-old Chevy, not a motorcycle."

"I think we've had enough of Oliver," said her mother, and she pulled into the driveway beside their house. The hats of three plaster dwarves gleamed on their next-door neighbors' front lawn. Kathy's was a common-looking wooden ranch house, painted pink by its previous owners years before, but it appeared to be almost magically silver in the light of the high full moon.

/2/

"Oliver said he'd come to Quincy to watch today," Kathy announced to her parents after a few general remarks had been passed about the morning's weather.

Her father shoved a picnic basket into the back of the car along with books for Jody and puzzles, games, and pillows for Bobby. "Who's Oliver?" he asked.

"Some boy Kathy met at the club last night," said her mother. "Kathy, you didn't say anything about him coming to Quincy."

"I forgot."

"Did you ask him to come?"

"No. I told him I was playing today, and he said he'd just come along to see. I don't mind." Kathy watched her parents exchange glances. Her father took off his glasses and wiped them on the front of his shirt. He squinted up at the colorless sky and said, "Let's go before it rains." *They're not going to say much,* Kathy decided, *because they don't want an argument before I have to play.*

"I know who he is." Jody took up the subject as she settled her little brother's head into her lap in the back seat beside Kathy. "I saw him last weekend at the club. He looks about my age."

"He does not," said Kathy. "Just because he isn't covered with hair like some ape doesn't mean he's twelve years old."

Jody smiled. "Kathy has a boyfriend!" she sang.

"Stop it, Jody," said their mother.

"Kathy's in love. Look at her blush!" Jody went on with plummy innocence in her voice.

"I'll bash you with my racket in another minute," said Kathy.

"Cut it out," said her father. "Who's your first round, Kathy?"

"I don't remember. Someone I've never heard of. Ruth something."

Kathy's mother moved a cardboard file onto her lap. She shuffled through it and removed a copy of the draw. "Ruth Gumm," she said. "What a name. Now, Kathy, if this Oliver person in any way affects your game . . ."

"Mother, please," Kathy said, looking sideways at her sister. Jody had rested a newspaper on Bobby's sleeping head. The newspaper was always present in case Bobby became carsick. As she did with all printed matter that came into her hands, Jody read it. She read at dinnertime, in cars, in the dark, and at courtside during Kathy's matches. What she read, she remembered, whether it was *Time Magazine*, Dickens, or the complete set of instructions for the Waring blender, and she had amassed in her head an encyclopedic amount of information of all kinds. "How do I love thee? Let me count the ways," murmured Jody.

"Cut it out," said her father.

"I was just reading from the paper, Dad," said Jody, hiding a smile.

"Kathy, pay attention," her mother directed. "Now you shouldn't have any trouble in your second round. Pam Carly is sure to win her first round too, but remember, she has no second serve at all. Come way in on it. Her last match . . . let me see. Her last match she double faulted twenty-two times. Keep the ball deep on her backhand side. She can't do anything with it."

"Is that the girl with the pigtails?" Kathy's father asked.

"Yes," said Kathy.

Jody hummed "If I Loved You" barely audibly.

"No problem with her," said Kathy's father. "Tomorrow you'll probably play Betty Schultz in the third round. Talk about her instead. Forget Carly, you'll beat her love and love. Schultz can trip you up. She beat Alicia deLong last January. Gordon's doing well with her. Let's go over Schultz and Alicia. You'll probably play Alicia in the semis."

Kathy answered her parents' questions mechanically, hardly hearing them. She argued with none of their advice and agreed to start deep breathing if she felt angry for any reason. She was aware of the constant passage of other cars around them. A horse van pulled into the slow lane in front. She wondered if the horse inside felt both bored and skittish at the same time, as she did. When she was sure Jody had stopped teasing, she fixed her eyes on Bobby's small pink face. Bobby suffered a never-ending string of colds and minor infections, which often meant bringing penicillin to tournaments in a thermos or packed in ice. He also had what her mother called "problems adjusting," although she never named what it was that he couldn't adjust to. His hobby was emptying tissue boxes or Band-Aid boxes or even his father's cigarette packs and stowing their contents, piece by piece, in hiding places all over the house. Kathy was forever coming upon bits of rolled-up tape or single M&M's behind a book or under a sofa pillow. Only Jody took pleasure in the ritual of finding Bobby's treasures. She exclaimed with glee when she discovered one, and Bobby still ran to her and hugged her and said it was her special present long after this game had stopped amusing Kathy and her parents.

"Keep in mind, if you make the semifinals next weekend, that Alicia is much stronger on Har-tru than clay," advised Kathy's mother.

"She won't be in the big tournament next month at the Newton Country Club," said Kathy's father. "That's your big qualifier, clay courts, honey, and you'll have a chance at Penny Snider and even Jennifer Robbins. It wouldn't hurt a bit to knock off numbers one and two."

"Let's do one thing at a time," said Kathy's mother. "Now Daddy will watch Alicia's first round. I'll be at

Pam's. When you're finished, meet us at the car for lunch, and we'll go over whatever notes we've taken. Then Daddy and I will both watch Shultz in the afternoon."

Kathy felt her focus shifting back to her father. "Dad," she said, "I can't guarantee beating Penny and Jennifer Robbins in July. Please don't make it sound so easy. Those girls are all more experienced than—"

"Honey," her father interrupted, "you don't have the perspective your mother and I do. In five years you won't even remember those girls' names. They'll fall by the wayside. Maybe you won't beat them this time or even next time, but you will sometime. It's a matter of putting things behind you one by one."

"There are thirty-one girls behind you now that were ahead of you last year at this time," Kathy's mother put in. "Daddy's right, see?"

"It may stop sometime," said Jody suddenly.

"Jody, that's enough," snapped her father.

"But what happens to Kathy if it does stop?" Jody persisted.

"Talent doesn't stop," explained her mother. "Do you think you'll ever stop reading books?"

"You don't have to hate anybody to read a book," said Jody dramatically. "You don't have to beat somebody else to the last page. You don't—"

"Jody!" shouted Kathy and her two parents all at once. Bobby woke and turned over, thumb in mouth in Jody's lap. Jody patted him and caressed his hair. They had a language together, those two. This thought occurred to

Kathy. Also she was speechless at Jody's use of the word *hate*. The word had never been used by Kathy, her parents, or anyone connected with tennis that she could recall since the day when she had first picked up a racket and begun.

Kathy recognized Ruth Gumm at once, although Ruth showed no sign of recognizing Kathy back. She was Marty's lumberjack, the lap swimmer. Ruth returned Kathy's warm-up shots disinterestedly. The day was of no certain temperature as the sky was of no particular color, and the flat light caused Ruth's round face to look especially blotchy. It fell without shadow on her earth-brown hair, which was cut in an odd Dutch boy style with bangs to hide the complexion of her forehead. Kathy asked Ruth if she was a new Plymouth Club member.

"Yeah," came the answer after a tiny pause.

"Where do you go to school?" asked Kathy.

"I don't know."

"You don't know?"

"We just moved here."

No form, Kathy calculated. *Marty's right. She is slow. I'll chase her back and forth a lot.* Ruth Gumm did have a completely untaught style. She hesitated before returning the ball, as if she were not quite sure what to do with it, but she managed at the last second always to hit it back.

"You play a lot where you come from?" Kathy asked.

"Some."

"Where are you from?"

"Out West."

"Well, you're a terrific swimmer," said Kathy cheer-fully. "I saw you last night. I wish I had such en-durance."

"I do laps."

Too much swimming is bad for tennis muscles. Kathy repeated this wisdom to herself but not to Ruth. "Are you ready?" she asked at last, stripping off her warm-up jacket.

"Yeah," Ruth answered, so vaguely that she suggested she would either never be ready or was always ready.

"You toss, I'll call. Rough," said Kathy.

Ruth flopped her racket indelicately on its side. "Smooth," she declared.

"I'm sorry, but that's rough," said Kathy.

Ruth peered at her racket as if she were trying to read something too difficult to be deciphered. "Smooth," she said again.

"Look at the strings!" said Kathy. "Anybody can see it's rough," as indeed anybody could have seen.

"It says smooth," Ruth insisted and pointed to the tiny word *smooth* printed on the throat of the racket.

"I don't care what it *says*. You had it strung wrong. It came up rough, and I serve." Kathy heard her own voice rise at the injustice and pettiness of this.

Ruth stood in the middle of her side of the court. She looked steadily but without apparent anger at Kathy. She did not give over the tennis balls. "It says smooth," she repeated.

"Oh, for Godsake, let's play," Kathy shouted, stamping

to her position at the base line. "Go ahead and serve if you want to be like that. I don't have all day." *Careful*, she warned herself. She took in three deep breaths, as she had been taught.

"Swearing is against USTA rules," said Ruth evenly.

"What?" yelled Kathy.

"Swearing is against USTA rules and against the code," said Ruth. She bounced one of the balls, and it dribbled away up to the net.

"Swearing!" Kathy's tone rose dangerously now. "What are you talking about? I'll tell you what's against the rules—delaying the start of a match and cheating on the call of a toss, that's what's against the rules! Go ahead. Serve! Play!"

" 'For Godsake' is swearing where I come from," said Ruth as if she were remarking on the height of the Rocky Mountains.

This time Kathy's voice could be heard several courts away. "Will you shut up and serve?" she shouted. "If you don't serve in ten seconds, I'm going to get a referee. I don't give a damn whether they eat . . . shingles where you come from, you stupid hick!"

"What's going on here?" a tired-looking woman asked, coming up to the back of the court. She seemed to take everything in in the space of a second.

"This girl," Kathy told the referee, "has cheated on the call . . ."

"Kathy Bardy," said the woman, "you are the one raising your voice. Calm down. You know about your temper, and you've been warned before." She took one uncomprehending look at Ruth, who still stood balls in hand. "Just play, Kathy," she said, and went away.

Ruth popped all three balls lightly over the net to Kathy. "You serve," she said. "I choose to receive."

"You *what?*" Kathy asked.

"I won the toss, and I choose to receive."

"You did not win the toss, and nobody chooses to receive," Kathy said.

"Me. I do." On the other side of the net Ruth Gumm stood ready. Neither crouching nor moving, she waited as if she expected to be thrown a softball.

Kathy paused before she served. She stared at the toe of her left sneaker and breathed again, trying to rid herself of what felt like a red-hot whole egg in her throat. She was shaking a little. *I'll murder her*, said one part of her. *Just play your regular game, and you'll finish her off in twenty minutes*, said another part. Her serve, harder and more vicious than usual, kept spinning out, and the more she fought to control it, the less controllable it became. Kathy lost her serve. She lost the second game and third. She lost the first set, taking only one game from Ruth. Time seemed both to gather itself into a single minute and to stretch itself endlessly as in a dream.

Kathy truly wanted to splinter her racket over Ruth's head, even if it meant she would be barred from tennis forever. She wanted to kill Ruth, to yank her ridiculous Dutch boy bangs, to physically attack her in some way so as to elicit a squeal of agony, some concession from her slow-moving soft body. Instead she fell twice, trying to reach Ruth's easy return of service. An obscenely ugly sore appeared on her right knee. This made things worse for Kathy, not because of the pain but because she prided herself on her graceful game, and now she felt as humiliated as a first-grader who has had an accident in front of the whole class. *Play your game! Wake up!* she ordered herself desperately, but she found herself constantly out of position, her legs moving like gelatin under water. Waiting for Ruth's awkward, accurate serve, she cried silently. She did not wipe her eyes to clear her vision except during breaks, when she plunged her whole face into a towel. *I'm in bed, asleep. This is a nightmare*, she thought, and she found she could not swallow.

During a break toward the end of the second set, when she was losing two-five, Kathy saw Oliver in the grandstand. He waved with a small gesture. She looked at him wide-eyed for a moment, as if he could bring her back to her senses, but did not return his wave. Instead she fastened her eyes on Ruth Gumm. Ruth sat with both legs apart, sipping at a can of soda. She showed no pleasure but seemed to be gazing at a distant object, six courts away.

At that moment a man's voice asked, "Which one of you is Ruth Gumm?"

Kathy turned, startled. A club official in a blue blazer was standing behind her, taking papers from a manila envelope and looking from Kathy to Ruth.

"She . . . she is," said Kathy, pointing as if Ruth were a rare kind of spider.

"Miss Gumm?"

"Huh?" Ruth answered, focusing her tiny eyes on him.

"I'm sorry," he said. "I'm afraid there's been a mistake in our bookkeeping." He passed a paper to Ruth. "We posted you this morning, but apparently you didn't pay us your entry fee. It was a mix-up, but without your eleven dollar entry fee you can't play in the tournament." He glanced at the score of the match. "I'll waive the rules if you can pay now," he added in a sad and hopeful voice.

Ruth said nothing. She stood and went over to her bag, which hung on the side of the empty umpire's chair. Out of it she pulled a white leather wallet and fumbled through it, dropping a dozen photographs and many coins on the court. "I don't have it," she said.

"Is your mother here?" the man asked kindly. "Someone?"

"Someone's picking me up later," said Ruth.

"Well, I'm very sorry," the man said. He reached for the paper and folded it in a knifelike crease. "If we break our rules, we'd have to do it for everybody, I'm afraid. Our accounting would be a hopeless mess. I'm very sorry," he said again. "Next time be sure and enclose a check or a money order with your entry blank. Okay?" He turned to Kathy. "You are Kathy Bardy?"

Kathy nodded, unable to find her voice.

"Good," said the official with a weak smile. He tried to joke: "At least we've got that straight! You get a bye, Kathy, and you play at three. Let me see." He consulted more papers. "Pam Carly just won. Three o'clock. Court twelve." He checked this fact off on his draw sheet, crisply put his paper back in the envelope, and marched away, his attention caught up by the match on the neighboring court.

In Kathy's wallet was a twenty dollar bill, paid to her

the night before. She heard some part of her mind trying to force her to stop the official, to pay Ruth's fee. She called herself a coward, yellow, without decency or a sense of sport. She knew she had cooled off now and that a kind gesture would give her a huge advantage. Ruth would not win one single game more. This she was sure of as she was sure of her own name, but after Ruth had squatted down to pick up her pictures and pennies, Kathy had still not moved, and in the end she did not interfere with this peculiar stroke of luck.

Oliver sat down on the bench beside Kathy. She hoped he wouldn't do anything sudden, like put his arm around her. That was all she would need should her mother come by.

"Why did they throw her out?" he asked.

"Technicality. Something about her entry blank," said Kathy. "I'm getting a headache. I'm going to get some aspirin."

"You would have lost," said Oliver.

"Well, I didn't," Kathy said, and an extraordinary vision came to her of finding nothing but a lump of coal in her Christmas stocking. At this time her parents arrived and had to be introduced to Oliver.

Oliver shook both their hands gravely, pushing his longish forelock out of his eyes. Whether it was his outsized glasses or his serious manners, Kathy didn't know, but Oliver produced a smile of such sympathy on her mother's face that she half-expected her mother to sing. "And Kathy tells me you're a tennis player too? You played out in California? That's wonderful," said her mother.

"Yes, ma'am," said Oliver as if he were addressing a queen.

"But then you must join the New England Lawn Tennis Association. You can play in our tournaments. It would be so nice!"

"I'll put you in touch with Bob Katz. He's the head of junior boys in this district," added Kathy's father, clapping Oliver on the shoulder with his rolled-up program as if he were a relative.

These offers and plans were expanded for several minutes until Oliver deflated them with the solid excuse that he had to work most weekends and weekdays. Then a lively exchange of pleasantries began about the insane cost of a college education. Kathy began to relax, thinking her match with Ruth would go unmentioned, when Jody, Bobby in tow, tumbled out of the grandstand and described in detail what had happened.

"Oh, Jody, can't you ever shut your big fat mouth?" Kathy whispered, but this didn't stop Jody. Her mother ended it all by telling Jody severely that Kathy was perfectly right not to pay the other girl's fee, as it would be a clear violation of club rules. She told Kathy equally severely that she'd better pull herself together for her second round, and she told Oliver very kindly that she'd rather he didn't watch that afternoon because Kathy had obviously been distracted by him to such an extent that she couldn't play properly. Kathy's mother was careful to make this appear to be Kathy's fault, not his. Her father winced throughout all this, but because he agreed, he only advised Kathy to "put it behind you."

On the way to the locker room Kathy found herself

alone at last, with a blinding headache. She made a sharp detour between two empty courts and found her sister, hidden under the grandstand, reading Dear Abby's column to Bobby.

"What are you trying to do to me?" Kathy asked.

"I thought you did a rotten thing. That's all," said Jody, not looking up from her paper. "You had the money."

"You're jealous of my tennis, that's what."

Jody snickered. "The last place you'd ever find me is out on some tennis court hitting a silly ball back and forth," she said. "I'm not at all jealous. I just don't think it's fair for you to get away with acting like a crumb." Bobby began to whimper. He stuck his fingers in his mouth and pleaded, "Read, Jody. Go on."

"You never watch any of my matches. You never pay attention to what's going on. How come you have to pay so much attention to this match? Tell me that," Kathy asked menacingly. "Just tell me that!" She grabbed the newspaper, tearing it, and threw it down.

"Please leave me alone," said Jody. "Let me take Bobby to the toilet and give him stuff to eat and read to him and sit here all day while you go out and play your game, and if you win, I'll do the same thing next weekend. We're all a big happy family pulling for you, Kathy."

"Oh, you suffer, don't you?"

Jody considered this as if it had been an honest question. "No," she said evenly. "But you do. I saw your face out there when you were losing. I've always seen you win before. This time you looked like you were holding out under a Russian torture session. And then you didn't make a move when the girl said she had no money. Wrong is wrong, Kathy."

"Mom says I was right, Miss Billy Graham."

"I know," Jody answered uncertainly. "I remember she liked it when the *Herald American* ran that interview and said you were lethally competitive. Maybe she brought us up differently, but I don't think so." She began folding the paper again, and when she had it right, she ran her fingers through Bobby's hair and continued with Dear Abby.

The sounds of tin lockers banging and not closing, girls laughing and yelling, swearing and calling to one another, one girl sobbing and then whining somewhere at the far end of the dressing room all went unnoticed by Kathy. She stood in a metal shower stall and let the hot water run over her for more than half an hour. Someone used terrible words and shouted that the combination on her padlock did not work. The padlock was slammed again and again into a hollow metal door. With identical rage and in time to the noise outside Kathy beat her head into the corroded tin wall behind her.

A little after six that evening Kathy alarmed her parents by insisting that if they did not drop her off at Julia's house her head would split into a million pieces. They finally agreed, although Kathy's mother did not like her dropping in on people, particularly the Redmonds, who had such good manners themselves.

"Kathy, honey, what happened to you?" asked Mrs. Redmond upon answering the door. "What happened to your leg? Have you had anything to eat? Is anything wrong? Are you all right?"

"I'm fine, thank you, Mrs. Redmond," said Kathy. "It's nothing," she added, indicating the bandage on her knee. "Just a strawberry. The courts were hard today."

"Well, come right in. You look like a kitten that swallowed a bumblebee. Did you lose your match today?" Here Mrs. Redmond signaled to Kathy's parents, who were waiting in the car to make sure that all was well. This she did with a hearty wave and a big grin, her silk dress swaying elegantly around her in the fine evening light. Then she closed the door and repeated her question.

"No," Kathy answered. "I won. I got a bye in my first round and won my second love and love."

"That's six to nothing, six to nothing?" asked Mrs. Redmond. She dropped her *g*'s slightly.

"Yes. I played well. I just came over to see if Julia wants to go over some algebra."

"Well, I don't imagine my Julia ever *wants* to go over a thing like algebra, but I know she'll want to see you, so just go on in the kitchen and tell Rose you're staying for dinner, and I'll get that lazy daughter of mine out of the bathtub." She paused. "But I know when something is wrong with my Kathy, and something is *wrong*," she announced with good-humored conviction, and she glided to the stairway and up, her chestnut hair and her skirt flowing behind her as if in a breeze.

As Julia's father was absent on a business trip, they ate in the kitchen instead of the formal dining room. Kathy never told anyone, especially Julia, and she didn't know whether it showed, but she loved this house, particularly the kitchen, with its glass-fronted oak cabinets and varnished brick floor and the huge pantry beyond, more than any place in the world. So much that she wanted at times to cry out to it and ask it to stay and be hers. Happily the Redmonds didn't consider her a visitor, and so she had spent much time in their house and at their table.

"Now, Julia," said Mrs. Redmond, dabbing at her mouth with a linen napkin embroidered with forget-me-nots, "your friend Kathy is upset about something, and I think we should encourage her to tell all."

"Jeez Louise, Mom," Julia said, seizing on a huge piece of steak, "maybe Kathy doesn't want to talk about it. You're not a shrink, Mom."

"That's all right," said Kathy. "I almost lost my first match to a real klutz today." She went on to describe how angry she'd gotten, but she did not go into the nature of Ruth's disqualification.

"But, honey, everybody loses sometime. See, you won after that. You shouldn't get so upset and fulminating over a little tennis game."

"Did your folks give you a hard time?" Julia asked.

"Yes. All the way back in the car. Mother blamed it on a boy, Oliver English, who was watching me. She didn't believe me that I'd forgotten all about him during the game."

Mrs. Redmond said she agreed with Kathy's mother that it was much too early to think about boys. "Your mother was an Olympic gold medal winner," she said, "and I'm sure she knows what she is talking about." But then Mrs. Redmond always agreed with everyone's mother, because this was one of her cardinal rules, and then she would turn around whatever the mother in question had said to suit her own point. Kathy reflected uneasily that sometime years ago she must have invented her mother's Olympic gold medal, or was it just Mrs. Redmond's inclination to speak glowingly of those people connected to her in some way? "This is delicious steak, Rose," said Mrs. Redmond.

"Thank you, ma'am," said Rose, who was listening to every word spoken.

"Mother," Julia said, "it's not just a little tennis game. If Kathy gets to the finals in this tournament and does well in the next one, she can have a shot at the number one and two players in New England. Then she's got a good chance of being ranked five or better in the next ranking period in order to get to the Nationals next year. She's even got a chance in a million of being asked this summer."

"Fiddle faddle," said Mrs. Redmond. "Kathy, that lovely filet mignon is getting cold on your plate. I want to see you eat every single morsel of it."

Kathy said she would try. After several more forays Mrs. Redmond pried out of Kathy that she was still furious about Ruth Gumm.

"Ruth Gumm! What a name! Now if what you say is the truth about her messing around and cheating with the rules or the code, then don't give it a minute's thought. As you can see, Providence interfered in the person of that club official. Just don't get so riled next time."

"Excuse me, Mrs. Redmond," said Rose.

"Yes, Rose?"

"It's not my place, of course, to say," Rose began, her ruddy cheeks shining in the soft overhead light. Rose's whole face took on the expression of a Celtic Gabriel. "But there's people named Gumm just moved next to where Cora works," she said. "Big sloe-eyed girl just Kathy's age. I would hate to say what Cora told me about them in front of Kathy and Julia."

"I'm sure Katherine and Julia are grown-up enough to hear what Cora had to say, Rose," said Mrs. Redmond cheerfully.

Rose polished the dish in her hand as if it were a piece of silver. "Cora says, and you know she never tells tales, that while the father is making rounds at the hospital, he's a doctor, the mother has been seen in male company, if you know what I mean, in the *daytime*," Rose added.

"Thank you, Rose," said Mrs. Redmond. "I'm sure that information will cause Kathy here to pity the poor girl instead of despising her."

It was difficult for Julia to sit upright in a chair. She much preferred to put her head on the seat of her father's old leather lounger, her light-blond hair streaming down to the floor. Her bare legs and feet she pointed to the ceiling. This she did the second her mother left the living room to "retire" into the last of her three daily baths. "You'll never guess what Mother's going to do," said Julia.

Kathy could not possibly guess. She sat herself properly on the deep gray velvet sofa and sank her bare toes into the flowers of the Aubusson carpet.

"You know that awful head Greco's making of me?"

"Yes?"

"Mother's paying for her to cast another one. She's going to put it on the mantelpiece. I told her how ugly it was, but she doesn't believe me. What'll I do if I ever have a boy over and he sees it? My God, I'll be embarrassed."

When Kathy had no answer to this problem, Julia said that the only solution she could see would be to steal the head off the mantelpiece in the middle of the night when everyone was asleep and glue it with Krazy Glue to the basin of her mother's bidet. Julia waited for Kathy to laugh. Her mother's bidet was always good for five or ten minutes of jokes. Kathy seemed to be in a dream. Julia slid gradually down onto the floor and, still upside down, scrutinized Kathy with care. "The Nationals are in Florida this year, aren't they?" she asked.

"Julia, come on. I don't have any chance this year. Next year maybe."

"But it would be fun, even next year, if we could go down and stay at Aunt Liz's house down there. You've never met Aunt Liz's two boys, have you? They're nineteen and seventeen, and they're both absolutely gorgeous. As a matter of fact, I'm madly in love with both of them."

The Redmonds' Siamese cat padded into the room. He walked soundlessly across Julia's stomach and leaped to the windowsill. The room darkened. Kathy gazed at the chair in the corner. It was called the bishop's chair because its back was high and pointed like a miter. When she and Julia were little, they'd pretended it was a throne and taken turns playing Queen in its red velvet depths. Mrs. Redmond never minded when they took massive pieces of sterling out of the silver closet to play Queen. She always said the silver was in need of polishing anyway. Over Rose's protests and threats of quitting Julia had been allowed to keep live and messy frogs and snakes in her room. Kathy's mother often said that Julia was thoroughly spoiled, but because whining and demanding had never been part of Julia's nature, this was hard to prove. "Kathy?" Julia asked.

"Sorry, I was just thinking."

"Do you have another migraine?"

"Yes. I've had it since this morning. After I lost to that big tub of lard, it just came on."

"Listen. I have just the thing. I just got a book out of the library. Sit down over here."

"Oh, Julia. Not another miracle theory," said Kathy, for Julia truly believed that the right combination of vitamins, hypnotism, and herbal liniments was the key to eternal life.

Julia brought out a thin book entitled *Cures of the Ancients*. Then she unscrewed two wooden drawer pulls from a highboy. "Here," she said, turning to a dog-eared page in the book and propping it up where the diagrams could be seen. "Now hold these two knobs—it says marbles but anything round will do—hold them against the base of your palms like this. Now pull your hair back from your face. My God! Kathy . . . what did you do to your head? You've got a lump the size of a golfball there!" Julia stared. "It's black and blue . . . it's green!" she said.

"I just banged it by mistake in the shower today."

Even as a little girl Kathy had seldom fallen or injured herself in any way, but Julia knew enough not to say that she disbelieved her. She got up off the carpet and closed the door on Rose in the kitchen and her mother upstairs, because Kathy had begun to cry openly and to repeat the same swear word over and over like an Indian mantra. To Julia the queer thing about Kathy's family was not that they bought discount shoes or saved coupons or were so tiresomely ambitious about everything. These facts Julia accepted because she knew herself to be more privileged than most people. The queer thing was that they were so very Yankee, so obviously opposed to affection of any kind, as if a kiss good night to someone over three and a half contained the seeds of a terrible destruction. For that reason Julia guessed rightly why Kathy had come, and she put away the book and the drawer knobs. Sitting on the sofa, she held Kathy's head in her lap like an injured puppy, as she had done from time to time before.

"Marty called," said Kathy's mother when Kathy let herself in at the kitchen door. Her mother sat at the Formica table, doing the bills. The unsteadiness of the fluorescent light, the plaid plastic backs of the dinette chairs, and the flesh-colored rims of her mother's glasses all united to create an impression of extreme weariness.

Kathy opened the refrigerator and took out a quart of milk.

"I told her how well you did against Pam. She was real pleased, although she said she expected it. She wished you luck tomorrow."

"Did you say anything about my first round? Not that it matters. Peachy Malone was blabbing about it all over the locker room this afternoon."

"We had a nice talk, honey. Marty told us what she thinks of you again. She says she's never run into natural ability like yours in all her years of coaching."

"Did you say anything about my first round?"

"I was thinking about that," said her mother, untying and then retying a shoelace. "Two days ago we had a customer come into the shop. You know that wedding Daddy did in Foxboro last month?"

"Yes?"

"Customer came in and wanted a full refund on the pictures. I know she had them copyprinted cheap somewhere. Some people will do anything. Boy, was I burned up!"

"What did you tell her?"

"What didn't I tell her! I was seeing red. Probably just like you with that Gumm girl this morning. You've got your mom's temper, honey, but just try and ride above it and, like Daddy says, put it behind you."

"I'll try, Mom," said Kathy, finishing off a glass of milk.

But Kathy was unable to do this, as she had one indistinct but terrifying dream about Ruth Gumm that night and another early the next morning.

Mirth and catcalling aside, the Plymouth Bath and Tennis Club Championships were taken quite seriously by most members. It was arranged as a round robin and dragged on for weeks, its schedule hopelessly complicated, and Marty, being the director, was as busy as the mother of a bride. Kathy was a shoo-in for the Ladies' Singles Championship, as she had won it easily the year before. This year Marty and Kathy would team up and try to take the ladies' doubles from Mrs. Rice and Mrs. Rosino, who had won it twelve years in a row. They were two ladies in their sixties who played a lovely old-fashioned game with the precision of a dancing couple on a Black Forest music box. The tournament counted for nothing, so Kathy's parents did not attend, but they did insist Jody earn twenty-five dollars as a ball girl, an amount Jody said she'd be glad to make pulling stumps out of their neighbors' garden instead.

Kathy had never played better than she had at the Quincy tournament, and so she had won the whole thing. This under her belt and school done, Kathy felt an excellent lightness of mind, connected too with the golden July days that spun themselves out like a reward and the gradual warming of the flinty blue North Atlantic. The thorn in her side was Mrs. Diggins.

Mrs. Diggins had seemed more saddened than appalled when she'd caught Kathy staring at the answers on Julia's conveniently slanted paper during the algebra final. She had been too kind to punish Julia as a coconspirator. With the air of a wise old nun who has seen and forgiven all kinds of wickedness, Mrs. Diggins tutored Kathy in algebra three nights a week. Three nights a week Kathy sat on Mrs. Diggins's nubbly brown sofa behind a card table, sweating over equations, trying to ignore the children in the neighborhood who shouted and laughed chasing their Frisbees and baseballs over the grass. This was impossible. Her mind would fly to the most insignificant fragment of conversation between unseen children outside the window and stay there until the speakers wandered away. Mrs. Diggins turned the air conditioner on loud and high to block the voices. It was an old machine and rattled away like a trash masher. Kathy counted in her head to the beat of a loose piece of metal inside it and confused herself further.

In Mrs. Diggins's opinion Kathy was obviously not stupid. She wasn't lazy either because as anyone could see, she really did perspire and gnash her teeth, chewing her pencil to splinters over the simplest problems. She had only to overcome her unreasonable hatred of mathematics and all would come clear, like the sunshine after a thunderstorm. Despite help from Oliver, Julia, and Mrs. Diggins, Kathy did poorly, since her hatred of math was as much a part of her as the color of her eyes. "If you would only apply yourself, Kathy," Mrs. Diggins told her forlornly, "with a fraction of the attention you give your tennis, you would at least pass the exam—at least have some basic comprehension of the course." But Kathy always lowered her eyes in real shame and promised to do better. Then a Monday, Wednesday, or Friday evening would roll around, and Kathy found herself opening Mrs. Diggins's front door with the apprehension she usually saved for the dentist.

One evening, when Kathy appeared, sunburned and flushed from four straight victories in the round robin, Mrs. Diggins asked her to sit in the wing chair instead of on the sofa. She offered her an anemic-looking glass of iced tea, which Kathy was too afraid to refuse, and then sat in an opposite wing chair. The fallow evening light suffused even the plastic ottoman on which Mrs. Diggins propped her feet with a delicate richness. "Kathy, do you know what growing up is all about?" she asked.

Kathy recalled a pamphlet, entitled *Growing Up and Liking It*, handed out at the beginning of freshman year. The pamphlet dealt with eggs and Fallopian tubes. To her dismay she also recalled that two nights before she had noticed a trace of blood on the sofa pillow when her lesson was finished. She'd done the only possible thing, and that was to turn over the pillow quickly when Mrs.

Diggins had left the room. *Oh, God*, she thought and wiped beads of sweat off her upper lip. "I'm sorry, Mrs. Diggins," she began, but Mrs. Diggins interrupted her.

"Growing up means doing things we don't like at least passably well," she said.

With thanks to God for the dark upholstery Kathy listened attentively.

"You are a wonderful athlete, Katherine, but you must do your schoolwork also. You will not pass freshman year unless you do. This will snowball into more failures. You cannot graduate from high school unless all your courses have been fulfilled."

"Yes, Mrs. Diggins."

Mrs. Diggins snapped on a lamp, as an intense shadow had covered the whole of her. "Your father said you must pass *just in case*. What do you suppose he meant by that?"

"Well, I guess in case my tennis . . . in case I don't do well enough at tennis. . . ."

"Exactly. And what you are doing, because you are young, Kathy, and think like all young people that nothing will ever really hurt you in life, is to coast. You are refusing to concentrate on algebra the way a baby refuses to eat spinach and throws it across the room when its mother's back is turned. Math is not your enemy, Kathy. Math is a tool, and you can make it your friend."

"Yes, Mrs. Diggins."

"I understand that serious tennis matches require a great deal of strategy and calculation, *sudden* calculation."

"Yes, Mrs. Diggins."

"Well, then you can calculate as well in algebra."

"Yes, Mrs. Diggins."

"I understand also that there is a certain amount of petty cheating that goes on in the early stages of the tournaments when there are no umpires. Is that so?"

"Sometimes, Mrs. Diggins."

"Do you ever cheat, Kathy?"

"No!" Kathy answered scornfully.

"But would you if you had to?"

"Never."

Whether Mrs. Diggins believed this answer or not, she didn't say. She took Kathy's glass and her own into the kitchen. Instantly Kathy inspected the sofa cushion. The spot had been discovered and removed. When Mrs. Diggins returned, she found Kathy working feverishly on the evening's lesson, her eyes wide and frantic like a guilty lawbreaker's. Mrs. Diggins smiled.

Oliver had become quite a fixture. Kathy's mother quickly sensed he was more like a brother than a boyfriend, and so she tried to fatten him up. Oliver nursed his injured pride at losing set after set daily to Kathy by wolfing down huge amounts of meatloaf and corn. At first Kathy had been unsure whether his questionable background would appeal or not appeal to her parents, but after the first two or three evenings she could tell that they felt more at ease with him than they ever had with Julia—a fixture in the house for almost nine years. "Lose again, son?" Kathy's father always greeted him at the door. This was a standard joke Oliver encouraged by pretending to laugh at it.

"Math is a tool. Math is my friend," said Kathy when Oliver walked into the kitchen. "I'm supposed to say that three times before I fall asleep at night." Kathy's father gave her a meaningful look, but he did not laugh as he had the night before when Kathy had told him about Mrs. Diggins and her positive thinking.

"Hi! Mrs. B., everybody!" said Oliver, and he plunged both hands into the everyday silver drawer as if he had lived in the house for years. He set six place settings around the kitchen table and announced he had a surprise for Kathy.

"What, what, tell me!" Kathy insisted.

"Diamonds, I bet," said Jody.

"Nope, but just as rare. Tickets to tonight's Yankee game at Fenway. Box seats!"

"Oh, Oliver!" Kathy yelled, and she began to jump like a child.

"No," said Kathy's father.

"What do you mean, *no*, Daddy? Come on, please," Kathy implored.

"No. Mrs. Diggins came into the shop today. She says unless you study harder, you might fail your final in August. I want you to put in another hour on your algebra tonight."

"And I say no too," said Mrs. Bardy. "Fenway Park is in a very dangerous part of Boston. I'm not having you two innocent things going out in the middle of the night and getting mugged."

Kathy could not meet this disappointment aloud without swearing unforgivably and landing herself, she knew, in unimaginable trouble. Through her teeth, which she'd clamped tightly together, she muttered a few words she'd heard from a Boston girl in the shower room during her last tournament. Her parents went on about the dangers of Fenway Park, and her mother forbade Oliver to go alone. Finally Mr. Bardy agreed to take the extra ticket and go to the game with Oliver.

Kathy said nothing during dinner until Oliver mentioned that he'd hit with and beaten a friend of hers at the club that afternoon.

"Who?" Kathy asked, still having eaten nothing.

"Eat," said Kathy's father.

"That girl who nearly beat you in Quincy in your first round. I beat her love and love," said Oliver with false snootiness in his voice, although he meant only to make Kathy laugh.

"Everybody beats her," Kathy growled. "She's lost six of her round-robin matches. Her doubles partner is a ten-year-old. The only girl who'd agree to play with her."

"Have you played her yet?" Oliver asked.

"I play her tomorrow. But Marty'll be around, and she won't dare pull any funny stuff." Kathy's voice was pure vinegar.

"Don't snap at Oliver just because you can't go to a silly baseball game," said Jody, cutting into a baked potato.

Kathy was about to throw her own potato at Jody when she felt her father put out a restraining hand. "I'm sorry, honey," he said, "but that's the way it's got to be."

"But it's the Yankees, Dad. Nobody can get seats. I promise I'll do four hours of homework tomorrow. Please, oh, please!"

"No, and your Mom's right about the two of you going to Boston alone."

"Take her, Mr. B.," said Oliver. "You can have my ticket."

"You have to think about algebra. The answer is no. You can watch it on TV if you finish your assignments."

"Big deal," said Kathy. Her eyes filled.

"Young lady," said her father, "first you apologize for that remark. Then you thank Oliver for being so generous. Then you learn something right now about responsibility. If you'd done your math right, I would have taken you both to Fenway, waited for you, and brought you back. It's your fault, Katherine, not your mother's or mine." When there was no answer to this, he continued in a gentler voice. "Honey, I want you to look at this. A saltshaker, right?"

"It's pepper," said Kathy.

"Never mind. I have four of them, right?"

"I can count to four, Dad."

"Two in this hand, two in this hand. Now I'm going to put two down here on one side of the ketchup bottle, and one on the other side of the ketchup bottle. The one in my hand, right here, I'm going to call x. Now pretend the ketchup bottle is an equals sign. What does x equal?"

"Two," said Kathy quickly.

"Oh, Kathy."

"Three!"

He slammed the pepper shaker down hard. "How can

it be two or three? Two and two is four. One and one is two. *X* is *one*, Kathy. Bobby could do that!"

"Then why don't they teach algebra in the first grade?" Kathy asked miserably.

"Go easy on her, Frank," said Kathy's mother. "Algebra isn't going to ruin Kathy's life. She's just got to get through it."

"How the hell is she going to get through it if you tell her it's not important?" her father shouted, throwing his napkin onto his plate. "She just may have to get a decent job someday and earn a decent living. Do you want her to be a waitress? Even waitresses have to add. You want her to be a maid someday?"

"Hush, Frank. I just meant tennis is the most important thing. This will pass. I did rotten in math when I was her age too."

"Well that's a fine thing to say," he growled, stabbing at his pork chop. "I wanted to give her hell for cheating on the final, and you wouldn't let me. Okay, I said, okay. Now you tell her it isn't important."

"All I said, Frank, was, if the teacher hadn't caught her, I wouldn't have gone running to the principal and told on her. What is important here? She has a gift. A marvelous talent. One girl in a million can play like Kathy. A million girls can count saltcellars."

"I think Kathy has a deep psychological resistance to algebra," Jody put in.

"I have a deep psychological resistance to know-it-alls," said Kathy, choking slightly. "Go ahead. Sink yourself into books all day, Miss Smart . . . aleck. What's that going to get you? By the time you're in college, you'll probably wear glasses an inch thick, and when you get to be fifty, you'll marry some creepy professor who looks like Henry Kissinger with dandruff and bad breath and zits on his—"

"Kathy, that's enough," said her father.

"I don't understand what's so hard about algebra," Jody went on as if nothing had been said. "Mary Beth Pendleton passed it, and Mary Beth's a real dip."

Kathy's potato hit her square on the forehead. Kathy was sent to bed. Instead she ran out the front door. She sprinted across the lawn, over the low privet hedge and the neighbors' barbecue, and then on to the next street. As she turned the corner she could see her father and Oliver looking after her from the backyard. Her father was shaking his fist in the air. She knew they wouldn't follow her, because they knew she could run ten miles with ease, avoiding streets and, should they take the car, losing them in an instant.

She jogged without effort, but no easy, light feeling came over her. She took shortcuts, over the Parrishes' lawn, past the Steins' enormous vegetable garden, trying to make sense out of the evening and out of Jody, trying to erase the picture of Mrs. Diggins as a secret trapper, soft as a patch of new grass on the surface but with solid mahogany punji stakes just below. Why were people like that always so right? Why did they always spot her dreadful little flaws, save them up like money, and present her with them, cooked and flavored like a perfect chowder of inconsistency, temper losing, and vile habits? "Math is a tool," she repeated to herself in rhythm with her pounding legs. "Math is my friend. Math is my friend. I can do it. Yes, I can." Mrs. Diggins, at the end of the lesson, had quoted extensively from a book about positive thinking. *I'll try it a hundred times*, Kathy thought, *and see what happens.* "I *can* do math, I *can*, I *can*, I *can!*" She repeated it aloud, and in a much less strident tone she murmured, "And, dear God, I promise never to forget to change a Tampax again if you will only let me pass algebra." Kathy could not fit this prayer into the proper positive sounding words, so she left off and continued with "Math is my friend! Yes, I can! Yes, I can!" Inadvertently she had come to the railroad, a distance of three miles and certainly a thousand *Yes, I can's* from her house. Neither the running nor the chanting had improved anything. No one was around to hear, as this was only a freight track overgrown with weeds. Kathy stopped. From the rawest depths of her senses she cried, "I hate you, Mrs. Diggins!"

She recalled looking in Mrs. Diggins's medicine cabinet in search of aspirin one night. In it was a sizable collection of false tooth cleaners, deodorants, and stickers-to-the-roof-of-the-mouth. "You toothless, heartless old bat!" Kathy bellowed. "Math is my enemy! No, I can't! No, I can't! I hate math and I hate you!" Kathy followed this up with a string of curses so colorful it surprised her that she knew them. As she trotted into an unfamiliar residential district she felt wonderful.

The two-story houses were narrow and set so close together there was barely room for a cat to slip between. They were all shingled brown and gray, some with little

pebbly maroon pinstripes on the shingles. The smell of
sour cooking was general to the street. People sat in
swings or on metal chairs. Jogging was not done in this
neighborhood, Kathy decided, so she slowed to a walk,
embarrassed by their stares.

She stopped near an old car, half off the sidewalk and
half on. Four boys were fixing it or tinkering with it.
They had the radio tuned to the Red Sox game. They
were not the kind of boys she usually said anything to in
school, but she wanted to hear the score and so she listened. The boys found this amusing, and one of them
asked her, snapping his gum in a yellow-toothed grin,
whether there was anything he could do for her. Afraid,
Kathy edged away as if he had been a German shepherd
and continued down the street.

"Hello, dearie!" said a voice, and Kathy jumped. She
glanced to the house at her side. In a broken rocking
chair sat an enormous man. His hair grew in odd tufts,
and two sleeping cats nestled in his lap. His clothes
were neat but sat on him queerly, as if someone else had
dressed him. The man rocked slowly under the light of
a single bulb, ignoring the swarm of moths and insects
that the bulb attracted. He was one of those, Kathy saw
immediately, who had never grown up and who never
would grow up, because she couldn't begin to guess his
age. One of those whom neighborhood people kept an
eye on but said was "harmless." There was also a woman
on the decrepit wooden steps. It was Miss Greco.

"Can I give you a hand, Miss Greco?" Kathy asked.
Miss Greco was struggling up the steps backward, haul-
ing what appeared to be a very heavy sack labeled Plas-

tilina Powder. The man in the chair made no move to help her, although the bag split more on each step. "Can I help you?" Kathy repeated.

"No, dear," answered Miss Greco, hefting the bag with a great flop and a massive cloud of ruddy dust onto the porch, "but why don't you come in and visit a minute? Have a glass of lemonade with Sam and me."

The steps and porch were covered with Plastilina dust. The front yard was filled with bits of broken crockery and hunks of plaster of paris. There were piles of empty cat food tins in and around the trash barrel. Neither the house nor the lemonade promised much, and because Kathy was in dead terror of the man in the chair, she said quickly, "Oh, I must get home before dark, Miss Greco, but thank you so much anyway."

"Another time, then," said Miss Greco and waved.

Kathy looped around a different street so she would not have to pass the boys and the car again. All the while she saw in her memory the strange man's eyes. They were pathetically crossed and yet seemed to stare directly at her over a dreamy red-lipped smile. Was he a son? A brother? *How cruel I was not to accept her offer*, Kathy thought, beginning to trot again. *Probably nobody ever visits poor Miss Greco. What a saintly person she must be. But I just couldn't do it. Oh, no.* Kathy shuddered. The cats and the idea of cat hairs in the lemonade and the thought of sipping from a glass that had also touched Sam's red wet lips froze in her imagination, and she began to sprint. Kathy was soon far away from the tumbledown houses and sour odors. *But Miss Greco has a decent job*, she tried to reason. *She's a teacher, after all. She has a decent job. Why does she live there?* Kathy's father's predictions about earning a decent living ran through her head ominously. The thought of the garbage in Miss Greco's tiny front yard sealed in Kathy a promise to triumph over both the first- and second-ranked girls at Newton and push herself not only into the first five but all the way to one. She passed into a more acceptable neighborhood and repeated the promise soberly and in horror. Then she changed direction and went on to Julia's house, as her parents would expect her to be there.

"I wanted to talk with you about this afternoon's match," said Marty without a *good morning*.

"Good morning, Marty," Kathy answered sweetly. She pushed her mop slowly and carefully over the pool deck until the white enameled boards shone. Overhead the sun was already brilliant in a cloudless blue sky. "It's a beautiful day," Kathy added.

"When are you finished here?" Marty asked.

"I have to clean up here at the pool. Then I have to make sure the lunchroom is clean. Then I'm on lifeguard duty for kiddie-swim until ten," said Kathy.

"You have a singles match at eleven."

"I know. Ruth was still doing laps when I came in this morning."

"You had trouble with her in Quincy, didn't you?" asked Marty, squinting and picking up a cigarette butt that had missed an ashtray.

"Don't worry about it, Marty." And then as an after-thought Kathy said, "Gee, she sure is strong though. She must have done twenty butterfly laps this morning. I went to change, and when I came out, she was still at it. Back and forth like some big flapping Saint Bernard."

"She does it every morning at six o'clock," said Marty. "Don't make fun of it. I'd like to see you out there at six with the ball machine."

"Okay, okay," said Kathy with a snort. "You wanted to talk about the doubles this afternoon?"

"Yes. Now I want you to watch Rosino at the net. When she goes to her right, she never—"

Mr. Molina's shrill voice interrupted Marty. "What do you think you're doing, young lady? You're supposed to have finished this whole area by now." And turning on Marty, he said, "A fine example you're setting! How would you like it if your ball boys and ball girls spent their time chatting away like magpies, frittering away valuable hours!" His clipboard quivered under his arm.

Marty grinned. She poked Mr. Molina lightly under the alligator on his puffy left breast with her racket. "Better get a bra, Fred," she said.

Kathy blushed as red as Mr. Molina. She scrubbed furiously, pretending not to have heard.

"I'm going to see to it that you're fired one day," he shrieked, pointing a finger to heaven. "Look at all that filthy green clay tracking up my deck! You're supposed to wipe your feet or put on clogs when you come to the pool area. I'm going to speak to the chairman about this."

"Better take some swimming lessons, Fred," said Marty. "I'll push you in the deep end when you're not looking someday!"

Mr. Molina disappeared around the corner of the

clubhouse. "You forgot to click your heels, Fred," Marty called after him. Then she resumed her description of Mrs. Rosino at the net.

"Marty." Kathy cleared her throat. She'd had a minute to think and to put what she had to say into the right words. "Mrs. Rosino and Mrs. Rice have won the ladies' doubles for years. They're so proud of their trophy. Neither of them has a chance at the singles. Why don't we play them and let them have it? It's only a club tournament."

"Are you out of your mind?" Marty asked.

"No," said Kathy, and she stopped scrubbing and leaned on her mop, toying with the strings with her toe. "I just think it's awful to get all worked up and plan strategy against two nice old ladies, that's all. It means so much to them to win, and it doesn't mean a thing to us."

"Now look here, my dear," said Marty. "I want you to listen to this and listen hard."

"I'm listening," said Kathy.

"Put down that stupid mop for a minute."

"Okay, Marty."

"Someday, my dear, you are going to be in a match against someone who wants to beat you like crazy, who can't beat you, and you are going to feel sorry for her, and if you do, you'll blow the match, and if you keep it up, you'll blow your whole career sky high, and you can kiss your future good-bye, right now."

"Okay, Marty, forget I said it."

"Do you know that Rosie Casals has never beaten Billie Jean King in a tournament of any size, *never*. They are very close friends all the same. Do you think Billie Jean lets Rosie have one once in a while to make her feel better?"

"No, Marty."

"Then this is excellent training for you. What are we going to do out there this afternoon?"

"Win, Marty."

"We're going to murder them and what else?"

"Watch Mrs. Rosino at the net, and when she goes to her right, slam it down her alley because she can't reach that shot."

"That's right," said Marty, "and cut the *Mrs.* Rosino. Until after we beat them, she's just Rosino to you unless you have to talk to her directly."

"All right, Marty, all right." Kathy picked up her mop again and began to work.

"I know how I sound," Marty went on. "I know what people call me when I'm not around, but if I were fourteen now, my dear, instead of thirty years ago, I'd have a million bucks in my future just like you. Be a nice guy all you want, but on that tennis court it's different. That's all I ask, and I ask it every single time you go out there. Okay?"

"Yes, Marty."

"Including your match this morning with that big tub of lard. No more repeats of Quincy. Keep your cool, keep your temper, keep your head. Ignore it if she tries to upset you. She plays tennis like an elephant. I want a score of love and love in that match."

"Yes, Marty."

At five o'clock Julia found Kathy hidden in an opening in the rocks behind a large pointed boulder at the end of the jetty. There was a rock "chair" there; on it Kathy slouched, one bare foot in a tiny sun-warmed pool of sea water that the high tide had deposited earlier that afternoon. Idly Kathy moved her bare toes through the bright green seaweed that waved in the natural bowl like gelatinous spaghetti. After a few moments had passed and Kathy had deliberately not turned her head to acknowledge Julia, Julia said, "Remember those? At my grandma's beach when we were little? There used to be so many little pools in her jetty. We put sand crabs in them and tried to keep them alive."

Kathy didn't answer.

"Remember when we entered the dead crab in the pet show and got an honorable mention?"

"I remember," said Kathy, implying that she didn't want to go on about it.

"Guess what Daddy's bringing home tonight! You've got to come over. He's bringing a dozen fresh eclairs, packed in ice, made this morning on the Champs-Elysées. He's taking the Concorde from Paris. We'll celebrate your doubles win."

"Oh, Julia, I'm not really hungry. I just want to sit here." Kathy continued to gaze out of focus at the rushing waves that broke over the mussels and squeaky brown seaweed below. She pulled off a bunch and began to pop the ends of the slippery tendrils.

Julia broke into her mother's drawl. "Well, whatever is eating at you, Katherine, you will always be a big heroine to every membah of this family."

"Oh, come on, Julia, that was years ago," said Kathy.

"Only three."

"Well, it was nothing."

"Dragging a hundred-pound person for nearly a mile is a pretty big deal."

"You didn't even weigh fifty pounds then, and it was more like a quarter of a mile, and if I'd had any sense at all, I would have left you where you were and run for help, and someone would have come much quicker in a car."

"Come on, kiddo, what is it?" Julia asked sadly. "You know you'll tell me eventually anyway."

"That girl beat me again this morning," said Kathy, popping all the seaweeds at once.

"You mean that stupid Judy Gumm?"

"Ruth."

"How could she beat you? Did she cheat?"

"No, she didn't cheat. There's a difference between cheating and gamesmanship. Cheating is calling a shot out when it's in. Gamesmanship is much worse. She diddled around forever on who won the toss. Then she delayed the match by saying she wasn't ready. Then when I got mad, she stopped the game and said I was swearing, which she couldn't possibly have heard. Then after every changeover she waited. Just waited until she was ready to come out. Only ten seconds longer than she should, but it drove me crazy. I tried to keep the ball on her base line. Tried to keep her running back and forth, but I kept hitting it out. Then my serve went—my toss. I started flicking my wrist on my toss. I tried to correct it and I double faulted five times. Then I kept dinking my serve instead of spinning it. I don't know. It was just suddenly over. She beat me four and three."

"Marty give you a rough time?"

"She glared at me with those eyes of hers and ordered me out of her office, as if I were a stranger."

"It just doesn't make any sense to me," said Julia, seating herself comfortably beside Kathy. "Do you know that big white whale swims a zillion laps every single morning before eight? Well, in the club swimming meet she lost the fifty yard freestyle by twelve yards to little Betsy Moran. I watched her. Betsy wouldn't be caught dead up at six in the morning. Betsy's not afraid of her."

"She *is* a great white whale," said Kathy slowly, "and she's got my number too, just like Moby Dick had Captain Ahab's number in English this year." Kathy sighed. "Marty's making me hit with her all next week, just to get her out of my system. You know what Marty said to me later? She said, 'That big ox has your number, my dear, and I'm the only one allowed to have that.'"

"You know what my mother says about Marty?" Julia began.

"Oh, Julia, you've told me three hundred times already what your mother says about Marty," Kathy snapped.

"You want me to leave you alone, Kath?"

"No. No. I'm sorry I jumped on you. Stay with me."

Julia leaned over and picked up a handful of seaweed herself. "People only have your number if you let them, Kathy," she said, "and boy, do you let them! Jody sure has it. She's always nicking your corners where it hurts. Marty has it. So does this dumb girl. Even Mrs. Diggins.

You said you could never look her in the eye again."

"Don't mention that. You promised not to mention it!"

"I promised I'd never mention it to anybody *else*. Jeez Louise, Kathy. You think you're the very first person in the history of the world who ever bled into something by mistake?"

"Don't talk about it. It makes me crawl to think about it. Last time I remembered it, I almost broke a toe kicking a chair."

"All right. All right. But, Kathy, wake up! You let everybody who wants it have your number. You let people rip you to pieces. You don't get even, you get mad, and you take it out on your own insides instead of on the other person. The trouble with you, Kathy, is you have no protective coloring."

"Protective what?"

"Protective coloring. Like the birds and animals in the woods. They never show themselves until they want to. You show all your cards, and everybody gets one up on you. You should tell Jody she's petty and jealous. You should make it clear to Mrs. Diggins you don't give a hoot for her sofa. You should make Marty come to you— *she's* got no future except you. You should match Ruth's tricks with your own."

"I can't play tennis like that. I can't concentrate. As for Marty, she's the greatest coach in the world for me. She makes me work."

Julia heaved a dramatic sigh and blew the air out between her pursed lips slowly. "Gee, Kathy, you must really want it so bad it hurts."

"Want what?"

"To *win*. To go to the top. Otherwise you wouldn't put up with all this garbage."

Kathy ripped off a new batch of seaweed. "I never thought of it that way," she said at last. "But you're right, you know. I do want it that bad. I want to be New England champion this year. I'd run to the North Pole barefoot if it meant I'd win. Stupid, of course, because I don't have a hope this year. But it's almost like a taste in my mouth. It's like when your mouth is parched and you see a big glass of water and you can just taste it. Promise you won't tell anyone I said that. I'd be laughed out of tennis if anyone heard me mention the New England championship."

Affectionately Julia placed her arm around Kathy's shoulders. "I don't think it's funny. I think you have a shot," she said. "By the way, I forgot to give you this. Marty gave it to me." Julia reached around to the back of the pointed rock and brought out a trophy labeled Ladies' Doubles Championship—Plymouth Bath and Tennis Club. Kathy and Marty's names were yet to be engraved on the plaque. Kathy grabbed the trophy, looked at it, and tossed it into the sea, where it banged once against a half-submerged rock and sank. Julia watched it go. "What's the matter, kiddo? What's wrong?" she asked softly.

"This afternoon," said Kathy, "I spent an hour beating the crap out of two sweet old ladies because Marty made me. It broke their hearts."

Kathy's mother placed a large platter of corn fritters and sausage on the kitchen table. Over it she distributed half a tub of margarine. "Eat!" she directed, smiling. "It's your big one, tomorrow, honey. You can win the whole shebang. I got your favorite dessert, Twinkies."

Kathy thought briefly about the eclairs she had eaten at Julia's house. "The Sox are in first place," she said, helping herself to six fritters.

"I wish we lived in Toronto," said Jody.

"Toronto?" asked her father.

"Toronto has a last place team," said Jody. "Kathy'd never root for a last place team, and then I wouldn't have to listen to all this baseball talk."

"What would you rather talk about, Jody?" Kathy asked. "Poetry?"

"Well, it wouldn't hurt," said Jody.

"How about 'Casey at the Bat'?" joked her father, but Jody did not laugh. When Jody appeared to be finished, her mother told her she could be excused without doing the dishes.

"Why don't you wait until I go to bed if you want to talk about something I shouldn't hear?" said Jody.

"Sometimes, Jody," said her mother with a sigh, "you are too smart for your own good."

"What is this?" Kathy asked. She wished Oliver were there. Oliver's presence usually modified things somewhat.

Jody left for the den with Bobby and with the parting shot that it looked as if everybody was planning a bank robbery.

"Well, you start, Frank," said Kathy's mother when the door to the den had slammed and the television's noise came through to the kitchen. Kathy's father shrugged and raised both hands in the air in response. Kathy guessed that her mother had won some argument with him but that parts of it remained unsettled. He lit a cigarette in an irritated way, shaking out the match as if it were as stubborn as an eternal flame.

"What is this?" Kathy asked again.

"Well," he said, "to be blunt and simple, Kathy, your mother has pulled some strings."

"That's a fine way to begin, Frank," said Kathy's mother.

"Well, that's what it is, isn't it?" he asked.

"You don't have to put it that way, honest to God, Frank."

"Okay, okay. Honey, Mom went to see Ken Hammer the day after Mrs. Diggins came to see us about your algebra. Remember?"

"Yes, Dad. Who's Ken Hammer?"

"Oh, Kathy," her mother broke in, "Kenneth B. Hammer is the superintendent of Plymouth public schools. You've seen his name on a hundred forms you've . . ."

"Okay," her father said. "Anyway. Your Mom went to see him. He's a real nice guy, by the way. Loves sports. Loves sports."

"Yes?" said Kathy uneasily.

"Well, Mr. Hammer is running for local office this November."

"Frank, you are putting the complete wrong slant on it. Why begin that way?"

"Well, he wants the Plymouth schools to have a big new sports complex. Tennis courts, everything. He has to raise a bond for it, of course."

"Mom," Kathy implored, "what does this have to do with me? I use the public courts at night, and we have courts at school."

"Honey," said her mother, "you've got to do well in the Newton tournament. Really well. If you can get through the finals, you'll make it into the top five. If Alicia deLong plays badly enough, you just might get invited to the National girls' fourteen and under. It's not likely, but you might. Mr. Hammer said it would be a great honor for the town, you know?"

"Yes?" said Kathy.

"Well, he was thrilled with the idea, as a matter of fact."

"But I was going to try and do that anyway," Kathy said.

"Of course, but while I was talking to Mr. Hammer I just mentioned in passing that you have, you know, a lot of pressure on you and all with your schoolwork, especially math."

"Yes?"

"He said there shouldn't be too much of a problem. He was so understanding. You know? He laughed. He had Mrs. Diggins when he was in high school. Can you imagine? Anyway, he said just to keep up the good work this summer with her. By the way, Mrs. Diggins will be going to a teachers' conference just before school starts. When you have to take the algebra final again? Anyway, he said you could take the final in the principal's office with him as proctor. Isn't that an honor? Superintendent of public schools! Anyway, he's going to set up a special program for talented and gifted students next year. Kids like yourself. You'll have a special course worked out and tailored to your special talents! His exact words. Isn't that nice?"

"I don't understand, Mom. What does this have to do with sports complexes and elections?"

"Nothing, nothing. Go get me the latest *Tennis Magazine* on the porch. I'll explain."

As Kathy got up and left the table she looked at her father, who had been so silent. He was cutting his sausage in smaller than usual pieces, using table manners he normally reserved for company, as if a stranger were present. When she brought back the magazine, her mother flipped through it anxiously and, finding an article on Tracy Austin, "Baby Tiger," read out a description of the courses that her California high school required: "English, Western Civ., whatever that is," read her mother, "Typing, Public Speaking, and Office Assistant. Office Assistant," her mother repeated for emphasis. "Can you just see it?" Kathy listened raptly. Her mother went on. "Anyway, you can't take stuff like that at Plymouth without being in the nonacademic course. You know, the General Course for the dummies? That wouldn't do you too much good college-wise, so you'll have to take regular classes next year, but Ken Hammer said he was going to . . ." Here her mother paused for the right words. "Well, you'll be in a brand-new program. Same courses but not the same work load, so you can practice and all."

"Mom, what does this have to do with Mr. Hammer's election?" Kathy asked.

"It doesn't have anything to do with that. Nothing!" said her mother. "That doesn't have a thing to do with you."

"Then how come you were talking about it, Dad?"

Her mother answered this. "Kathy, Mr. Hammer is also going to have some work done in Daddy's lab, that's all. That's Daddy's business, and that's why he was talking about it. Daddy's doing Mr. Hammer's campaign photography and printing up his literature at the shop. It's a nice job for Daddy. It doesn't have anything to do with this. Won't it be nice if he gets elected and the school gets six new courts, though?"

"I don't need them," Kathy said. "I play in Swampscott anyway because Marty's there. How come . . ."

"By the way," her mother interrupted, "I spoke about this to Marty, and she thinks it's a terrific idea. Fabulous. It's what you deserve, honey. You're never going to have to kill yourself over the books again. Isn't that great?"

"I guess so," Kathy agreed. She watched as her father left off eating rather quickly, put his plate in the sink, and disappeared into the living room. She tried to make sense of the many threads of things she'd heard. Finally she said, "A special program for talented and gifted kids like myself."

"That's what he said."

"Well, there's Jimmy Morrow, who's a junior and all-state basketball, but there *aren't* any kids like myself, Mom." Kathy looked behind her chair to where her mother stood at the sink, her arms elbow deep in suds.

"You bet, there's no one like you," her mother agreed.

"But I didn't mean it like that, Mom," Kathy began.

"Kathy, you know what?"

Kathy expected an off-putting remark about being too young to grasp certain things. "What?" she asked cautiously.

"You're going to be New England champion this year, honey," said her mother without turning around.

Later on in the evening, after Kathy had settled herself in front of the television, Jody mentioned Mr. Hammer's visit that afternoon. "Mom and Dad aren't charging him for the campaign photographs and printing, you know," she said.

Seated on the bench for what Kathy knew would be her last game of the afternoon, she relaxed, and she smiled for the first time that day. She smiled because she had won her first round easily and was beating Betty Schultz in the second round by a score of six-one, five-love. She smiled because Ruth Gumm had been placed way down the draw from her with a first-round match against the number one player, Jennifer Robbins the great. Kathy smiled at the sixteen beautifully swept red-clay courts, pride of the Newton Country Club, difficult for some of the girls, easy for Kathy's game, and she smiled because Oliver was watching from somewhere, not wanting to show himself because of Marty. Marty was also watching from somewhere. She had come to Newton on official club business, but she stood under the grandstand at times and behind a speaker's platform at other times, keeping track of Kathy's games. Had Oliver sat up front and had Kathy done badly, Marty would have forbade his presence forevermore.

Betty Schultz gasped for breath on the other side of the net. Her game had gone completely sour. Not wanting to look arrogant, Kathy hid her smile from Betty, but Betty didn't notice anyway. Later in the locker room she would fold up and cry. Half the girls did that, some in privacy, some in front of everyone. Betty had called three or four of Kathy's serves long when they'd been right on the line. Kathy had seen where the tape had puckered, but she didn't care. She drank a sip of water. Betty had lost the last fifteen points. Kathy stood and walked out to the base line, ready to receive Betty's newly cautious serve. Double fault.

Poor Oliver. Between points Kathy tried to locate him in the stands. A few nights before, when they were sitting in the house babysitting for Bobby, Oliver had admitted that it made his skin crawl to lose to Kathy, a girl, and three years younger than he. He didn't want to sound like a male chauvinist pig, no. He only wanted to get his feelings out, for feelings, after all were very important, and people had to get them out or they became raving neurotics. Then he had done all her algebra homework for her because she'd been lazy. When Kathy had wished aloud for some ice cream, Oliver had driven down to the corner and had come back with three double-decker cones. The third he finished himself since Bobby fell asleep in his lap after two bites. Half of Kathy's attention had been drawn to the Red Sox game on the television. The other half was on Oliver, who had sunk far back into the Black Watch tartan Naugahyde sofa, Bobby snoring adenoidally into his pants legs. "I want you to marry me, Kathy," he had said at that moment.

Betty Schultz hit a weak second serve at Kathy. Kathy belted it down the line. The shot fell in by an inch. The match was over, and the two girls shook hands solemnly at the net. Oliver was first on the scene. "Congratulations!" he said with brightness in his voice. Kathy thanked him and plunged her face into two icy handfuls of water.

"You should see yourself!" Oliver laughed.

A small mirror hung from the umpire's chair. He turned it so that Kathy could see her face, which was streaked like a clown's with red clay. He laughed again and said, "Don't wash it off. I like your face all dirty!"

"Oh, Oliver, don't be silly," said Kathy, and she removed every speck of clay with a towel.

"You do think I'm silly, don't you?" Oliver said. "Did you think I was awfully silly Tuesday night?"

"Oliver," Kathy answered, "I am fourteen years old. I can't think about marrying anybody. I'm not even allowed to date!"

"Did you know," Oliver asked wistfully, "that in the fourth century the Empress Tsu Chu was married when she was five?"

"Hello, Marty," said Kathy. "Hi, Mom."

Kathy's mother was full of congratulations and enthusiasm for Kathy's easy win. Marty waited for Mrs. Bardy to finish and then she said, "Betty Schultz is small potatoes and Kathy knows it. Tomorrow you'll have to play Alicia deLong in your third round and then probably Susie Chan. She's a lefty, remember that."

Kathy answered in a singsong, "I know, Marty."

"If Susie Chan has a good day, she can beat anybody," Marty warned.

"She usually doesn't have good days," said Kathy.

Marty toyed with the blue and yellow piping on her immaculate white jacket. "She had a good day today. She beat Daisy Wall this afternoon very solidly, and that was with a nasty case of poison ivy," said Marty.

"Okay, Marty, I can handle Susie Chan," Kathy answered. Her mother was fidgeting, wanting to get on with something, Kathy could see.

"Just don't get too confident is what Marty's saying," her mother added. "Now listen. Bobby is sick again. Jody's with him in the car. We've got to get out of here. Just put your sweater on and hurry with your shower. Marty, can we give you a lift home?"

"Oh, no thank you," Marty answered and wandered off to what mysterious business she had at the Newton Country Club.

"Oliver," Kathy heard her mother ask as the two of them left, "would you mind driving the car around to the front gate while I get Kathy a milkshake? It'll save time."

"Done," said Oliver. He took the keys.

"Oliver, you've been worth your weight in gold to us this summer," her mother went on. "Especially when Frank's not here. I'm thinking of adopting you."

"Oh, no!" Oliver answered completely without shame. "Don't do that. Then I can't marry Kathy!" She watched both her mother and Oliver explode in laughter at this remark. She shook her head and found herself wondering where it was that Marty went after a tournament, after the club was closed. Did she have anybody in her life? Did she own any clothes that were not white?

Kathy stepped into a shower stall. She forgot to excuse herself when she found it occupied. She was only able to cry out, "My God! Susie, look at you!"

"Get away!" said Susie Chan, laughing. "It's boiling hot. It's supposed to help." Great clouds of steam and splashing water poured over Susie's arms, which, Kathy could see well enough, were a mass of tiny yellow blisters. Hundreds of them covered her forearms and wrists and had made their way over the backs of her hands to the knuckles. "Do me a favor, Kathy?"

"Sure, anything."

"Get that bottle of brown gunk out of my locker. It's one forty-eight. Just pour it all over when I take my arms out of the water."

Susie did not flinch when Kathy, spilling most of the contents of the bottle on the floor, quickly poured the medicine all over her ghastly-looking arms. "I'm still going to beat you tomorrow," Susie said between clenched teeth. "If you beat Alicia. Alicia's not playing well these days. Pam Carly says she's in love and it's ruined her backhand."

Kathy laughed. "Who's your morning round?" she asked.

"Don't know. Haven't seen any results. It's early, but I'll be up for you at two o'clock. I'm getting a cortisone shot tonight."

Kathy wrapped both of Susie's arms in towels according to the instructions on the bottle. The towels turned tea colored immediately. "This is terrible," she said. "I'd be the world's worst doctor. I'm feeling faint."

"Don't faint. It's not fatal."

"It looks fatal," said Kathy. She got into the next shower and took three deep breaths, as she could not look at people who were ill or hurt. She thought briefly of Jody, who thrived on cuts, splinters, and burns. Jody loved anything that required soaking, Merthiolate, particularly intricate bandaging, or the sterilization of sewing needles.

"Short of throwing a match," said Susie, "let me know if I can ever help you out."

"You can," said Kathy, her eyes closed against the dreadful towels and the smell of whatever was in the bottle. "You can give me a ride tomorrow. My little brother's sick, and I know my mom would like to keep him home if she can." Kathy pictured Susie's face behind her closed eyelids. It put her suddenly in mind of the

Empress Tsu Chu, married at the age of five. "Susie," she asked, "how early do Chinese people get married?"

Kathy's mother allowed Oliver one glass of beer during dinner. He raised it and drank a toast to Kathy's success. This did not fool Jody, who observed that love and jealousy went hand in hand, and jealousy always won out. In his heart of hearts, Jody went on, Oliver did not want Kathy to win because he was a male and males could not stand females who did better than they, especially in sports. Oliver was not outwardly disturbed by this. He cut off Kathy's rejoinder. "Okay, Jody," Oliver asked, "you are Kathy's own sister. Are you hoping she beats Alicia and Susie tomorrow? Are you hoping she'll win the whole thing, because she can, you know. By next Thursday Kathy can be the hottest thing in New England tennis."

"She already is," said Jody over a piece of corn.

"Answer the question, Jody," said Kathy.

Kathy's mother broke in, saying it was a night to celebrate and not to fight.

"I'll answer it," said Jody.

"Eat your corn," directed her father.

"You can say something if it's nice," said her mother.

Kathy watched her sister carefully. There had been a time when Jody had copied everything Kathy had done. She had slept in Kathy's bed when she'd been frightened by thunder and lightning. They had wandered together on long summer days, had poked at snakes hidden in streams, knife grass against their bare legs. They had collected turtles, moths, and pieces of mica. Together

Kathy and Jody had rescued baby birds and watched them die, had protested bedtimes, and had been taught not to swear, but it seemed to Kathy at this moment that it was her sister, not she, who had grown knowledgeable and adult, quite suddenly, like the mushrooms that materialized on the lawn when no one was looking. "Out with it, Jody," said Kathy.

"If you don't win," said Jody thoughtfully, "you'll go to pieces."

"I will not."

"I think you will. I think you'd better win, Kathy, because if you lose, you won't ever have the heart to go after something like this again. I hope you get to Wimbledon someday." Here Jody stopped.

"Because you don't think I'll be good at anything else?"

"I don't think you care about anything else. There's a difference." Jody seemed puzzled by her own thoughts. "The answer to your question is yes. More than anything I can think of, I want you to win, Kathy, but not for the reason you want me to."

"Oh, Jody," said Kathy with a sigh, "I just wish you'd plain out and out root for me for a nice simple reason for a change."

"God preserve us from your Doctor Freud, Jody," added Kathy's mother. "There's the phone. Everybody be quiet. It's the doctor calling back. He thinks he's located a brand-new antibiotic for Bobby's ear. I have to go to Norwood or someplace to pick it up, but at least the poor kid won't have to swallow that gunky pink penicillin three times a day."

It was not the doctor. "That was Mrs. Chan," said

Kathy's mother when she returned to the table. "Susie's got blisters the size of eggs between her fingers. She can't play tomorrow, but Mrs. Chan's going to give you a ride anyway. Susie sends her best and wishes you well with Alicia."

"I guess I don't play her then. I wonder who I will play. Who was Susie's morning match, her third round, supposed to be?"

"Robbins," said her mother, "unless Jennifer lost to Jackson, Karen Jackson, which isn't likely."

"Jennifer Robbins is out of the tournament," said Jody, "and Karen Jackson played horribly today. She lost her second round match."

"How do you know? You never pay any attention," Kathy interrupted.

"While I was waiting in the car with Bobby, Peachy Malone came by. She brought me a Popsicle and she told me."

"Well, I wonder who I play then."

"Ruth Gumm," said Jody casually.

"What? That's impossible," said Kathy. "You must be wrong. She couldn't beat Jennifer Robbins. No one can beat Jennifer Robbins.

"She didn't," said Jody patiently. "You weren't listening. She was lucky. Jennifer had to leave the tournament this morning to fly to New York for a funeral or something. In Ruth's second round she beat Karen Jackson. Karen just had a bad day. She hurt her thumb on a Coke can pull, and her game went out to lunch. Ruth squeaked by in a third set tie-breaker. So, since Susie Chan's defaulting her morning match, if you beat Alicia in yours, you'll have to play Ruth in the fourth round tomorrow afternoon. Look at the draw if you don't believe me." Jody twirled her fifth ear of corn onto a corn holder. "Holy cow, Kathy, you look as if you had a tarantula on your plate!"

"Kathy, eat," said her mother. "So what? You won't have any trouble with Ruth Gumm. You told me Marty made you hit with her for more than a week every day and that you won every single game. You've got her in your back pocket."

"Wasn't true, Mom. I lied."

"You mean she's been beating you again? That dumb ox?"

"Marty was furious with me. I couldn't tell you, Mom. I was too ashamed."

Kathy's mother considered for a short moment. "Well, you're going to have to do something about it. That's all. Right now. Stop crying. You're not a baby. After dinner you go right down to the public courts . . . what's been your worst shot, your worst fault with Ruth? What?" Her mother's voice tightened.

"Serve. I don't know. I get tensed up and my toss goes. Keep trying to ace her all the time. Second serve dribbles away. I don't know, Mom. It's like a cloud descends on me when I have to play her."

"You go right down to the night courts and you serve it out of your system. Do you understand?"

"I have algebra, Mom."

"Forget algebra."

"Now wait just a minute," said Kathy's father. "I say she goes to algebra and that's final."

"After algebra," Kathy's mother continued. "You go down there, and you serve until you've got Ruth Gumm out of your system for good, and then you tell Joe Potter to put on the ball machine. She plays like a ball machine anyway—at least her speed is about as challenging. My God! A dummy, a nothing like that scaring you! It's ridiculous. If you go into the finals in this tournament, you'll have a chance at an invitation to the Nationals. Marty told me today. She heard it straight from Caroline Collins of the NELTA. They're not pleased with Alicia deLong's record this summer at all. The Nationals, Kathy! Are you going to blow that chance over some stupid fat pig who can't even play tennis?"

"I wish I could do it in the morning, Mom. At five o'clock?"

"What for?"

"Nothing. I just . . . the Sox are playing the Yanks, and I wanted to relax and see it on the tube."

"No, it's not on," interrupted Jody. "There's a news special instead."

"You look here, young lady, and you listen. Stop looking at your feet. Look at me in the eye."

"Yes, Mom."

"Your Dad and I haven't spent God knows how much on this tennis game of yours for the sheer fun of it alone. You have an obligation here, and you are going to practice. All right?"

"Yes, Mom."

"All right."

There was a silence, and Oliver cleared his throat conspicuously. "Jigger Marantz with baggy pants," he said.

"What?" Kathy asked, her voice trembling a little. She had lost all her appetite.

"Baseball trivia," said Kathy's father. "It's nothing, honey, nothing at all."

"Who has baggy pants, Oliver?" Jody asked.

Oliver glanced at Kathy's father. "Sorry," he said.

"What are you talking about?" Jody asked.

Mr. Bardy considered for a minute. "Jigger Marantz was a ballplayer many years ago, Jody," he said. "You don't want to know about ballplayers. You hate baseball."

"I'll look him up in the library," said Jody.

"Oh, God, Jody, all right," said her father. "Well, Marantz was an outfielder for the old St. Louis Browns. He was a bench warmer, really, never hit above two hundred. Anyway, there used to be a big pitcher in those days, Walter Johnson was his name. They called him the Big Train. He was probably the best pitcher in baseball history. Hall of Famer. Most of his records still stand to this day. Well, the only guy Marantz could ever hit was Johnson, and the only guy Johnson was ever afraid of was Marantz. When Johnson pitched in St. Louis, the fans went crazy yelling 'Marantz, Marantz with baggy pants!' Johnson was stupid. He let the guy get to him. He should have burned his fastball right down the middle and blown the guy away, gotten him out of his system. Instead he used to pitch around him, walked him and let Marantz hit home runs off him. Anyhow, the whole confrontation was never resolved. Marantz was hurt bad one night in a barroom fight. Blinded. Someone threw him into a mirror. He never played again."

"Did Walter Johnson do it?" Kathy asked.

"No, honey. As far as I know they never caught the fellow who did it. Johnson was pitching in another city that night. It's a very famous baseball story, though," he added in a hopeful voice, sensing the chill that had settled around the table. At that moment the doctor called and the front doorbell rang.

Kathy sat unmoving at the kitchen table. She pressed her fingernail along the line of checks on the Formica surface. Plans and arrangements flew in and out of her attention. The doctor wanted to take a throat culture, and so her father and Bobby were dispatched to the clinic. The druggist in Norwood would stay open until her mother arrived to pick up whatever miracle drug had just come on the market from Canada, or was it Germany? Yes, her mother would drop Oliver at the club so he could help Mr. Molina with the fiftieth anniversary cocktail party. Jody would stay home and do the dishes. Kathy was reminded that she'd left her racket in the garage and her algebra book under the bathroom sink.

Suddenly Julia walked into the kitchen carrying a large cardboard box. "Mom's waiting for me in the car, I can only stay a minute," she began. "Where's everybody going? Kathy, what happened? Did you lose today?" Julia asked, setting her box down in the middle of the table. "You look as if you'd eaten a bad clam!"

The kitchen was suddenly empty except for Julia, Kathy, and Jody. "She just found out she has to play Ruth Gumm tomorrow," said Jody. "What's in the box, Julia?"

"Well, it doesn't seem like the right time for it," said

Julia, staring at Kathy's snow-white face. "I just brought it over for a laugh, but nobody seems to be in the mood for a laugh."

"I am," said Jody, and she unwrapped the parcel herself. "What in creation is this?" she asked. "It looks like the Cro-Magnon man at the Museum of Science."

"It's supposed to be me," said Julia. "Miss Greco made it. We just went over to pick it up at her house. You never saw such a mess in your life. Cats, cat food, dust all over the stairs, broken dishes." Cast in attractive bronze, the head gazed out at them from its box. "But the funniest thing is," Julia went on, "I could never figure out about Miss Greco's heads until tonight. She has this son, or relative. His name is Sam. He's very scary-looking. All her heads look exactly like Sam. Kathy, where are you going?"

"Algebra," said Kathy.

"But wait! We'll drop you off. Mom's outside."

"It's okay," said Kathy. "I'll run over." And she left instantly, with no books.

The following evening Mrs. Chan brought Kathy to her front door. Hearing the car in the driveway, Kathy's mother came running out with a ten-dollar gift certificate from the photo shop in her hand. Kathy cringed. She could see that Mrs. Chan was insulted—she had given Kathy a ride as a part of an exchange of kindnesses. She had been on her way to Boston anyway. She did not want to hurt Mrs. Bardy's feelings too much, and so she just smiled and returned the gift certificate, saying she didn't have a camera. When Mrs. Chan drove away,

Kathy told her mother that it was tacky to pay people for favors.

"And I know," said her mother, "just where you pick up words like *tacky* and ideas like that."

"Mrs. Chan took me because Susie promised me a ride. The Chinese are very big on promises, Mom. By trying to give her that money you made her lose face."

"It wasn't money," said her mother, opening the front door. "Now how did you do?"

"I won."

"I knew it!" Her mother's face exploded in a wide grin. "Kathy won!" she yelled to the rest of the family, who were in assorted places in the house.

"Mom, you embarrassed me in front of Mrs. Chan. Now she'll tell Susie, and Susie will tell Peachy Malone, and she'll..."

Kathy's father trotted down the stairs and into the living room. He put his cigarette in an ashtray, spread his arms, and hugged Kathy in midsentence, "You're my girl," he said. "I knew you could do it. I knew it. I knew you'd just go out there and beat the daylights out of that silly girl."

"Dad," Kathy said, but he went on.

"I knew it when I saw your face at the table last night, honey. After I told that Jigger Marantz story. There's nothing like a good story to show a good example. You did just what Walter Johnson, a big grown-up man, couldn't do. You went out and overcame fear. You went out there and said *can do*, and you made it happen all by yourself because you knew you were the one who had to do it. From this day on, honey, I know you'll never let anyone get a whammy on you. This calls for a drink!"

"Dad," said Kathy.

"Yes, honey, come on in the kitchen. Mom's got dinner almost ready. You know what I'm going to do? I'm going to send for tickets tonight for the next Yankee game at Fenway, and I'm going to take you and Oliver. You deserve a celebration for what you did. I'm—"

"Dad, please," said Kathy. She went into the kitchen after him and waited for him to pour a glass of whiskey. "Dad," Kathy said, "Ruth didn't show today. I didn't do anything big. I beat Alicia this morning, but I was so jumpy it took me three sets to do it—ten match points! I waited for Ruth at two o'clock, but she didn't show. I told the umpire I wouldn't take a default even after an hour and a half had passed. I waited till three forty-five, and then Mrs. Chan came, and I didn't want to hold her up. The girl never showed, Dad. I was lucky this time. I didn't have to face her, so I didn't do anything great. I just accepted her default."

"Oh," said her father in a disappointed voice. "Still"— he raised his glass—"here's to the round of sixteen tomorrow anyway. It was real sporting of you to wait. That shows you were up for her. You would have beaten the pants off her."

"It wasn't necessary," said her mother. "The NELTA has rules about players being on time. Kathy should have accepted the default after the regulation ten minutes. It may sound picky of me, but champions aren't champions because—"

"Mother, would you stop," Jody interrupted. "Kathy did something nice for once. Champions, whatever that means, are on top because they're good. Not because they nickel and dime people on a bunch of silly rules. Here's Oliver. Let's eat."

Oliver walked directly to the kitchen sink, washed his hands, grimaced, and then inspected his fingers in the light. "Steel wool," he said in a self-important voice. "Did you hear what happened, by the way?" When everyone said no, Oliver explained that he had spent the entire day scrubbing the sides of the swimming pool with six other lifeguards. "Didn't you hear?" he asked.

"No, what?" said Kathy.

"Ruth Gumm drowned this morning."

"What?"

"Molina found her. The police said it was death by drowning."

"The police!"

"He had to get the police. The doors to the pool enclosure were locked from the inside. Apparently she had a key because she did laps before the club opened. She always locked the doors from the inside. Molina had to get the cops to break down the door. He found her in the shallow end. They drained the pool. He tried to revive her, but the doctor said she'd apparently been dead about an hour and a half. My hands are full of these damn steel wool fibers. It's like a million splinters. They won't come out."

"That's a shame about the girl," said Kathy's mother. "I'll get you some Lava soap, Oliver."

"See what happens when you swim alone?" said Kathy's father. "A damn shame. Fourteen years old."

"But she was such a fantastic swimmer," said Kathy.

"Good swimmers don't just drown. Why did she lock the doors from the inside?"

"Molina made her in case anyone came by to rape her. He said she always opened up at eight o'clock when he got there. He was really upset. Last night when they closed after the cocktail party, I watched him lock up. You know his routine? He locks the door, and then he unlocks, and then he locks it all over again and says, 'The door is locked!' like that. He's been at the club thirty-three years, and they've never had a drowning before, even in the ocean. You'd have thought it was his kid the way he was carrying on."

"Well, accidents do happen," said Kathy's mother. "Try some Vaseline, Oliver. Look at that poor girl, that skier who was paralyzed from the neck down. They did a book on her." She put a plate of franks and beans down in front of Kathy. "Honey, don't make a face like that," she said. "You'd think I'd given you a dish of worms."

But Kathy's mind was far away, uneasy, dreaming as if she were deeply asleep. She had it pictured that all the roofs had been somehow removed from all the buildings she would ever find herself in for the rest of time. Individual rooms, with walls only, appeared like so many floor plans. Above the rooms, drifting, watching every move she would ever make, Ruth hovered in a kind of heaven that sat about a hundred feet above the world. She was not transformed in any way in Kathy's mind. No wings decorated her shoulders. No light emanated from her body. Her complexion was still uneven, her hair still in a Dutch boy cut. She waited, showing no expectation, much as she did for a serve.

/ 5 /

Julia's Aunt Liz was always called the Bullet Aunt. This was because as a child in her father's dry-goods store Aunt Liz had stepped right into the path of a holdup man's bullet, which had been intended for her father. After that Aunt Liz had been visited every day in the hospital by the entire seventh grade of Valdosta Grammar School until their prayers took hold, the bullet ceased to infect, and Aunt Liz lived to tell the tale, which she did often, even though all this had happened thirty-odd years before.

Kathy had never heard this story from the lips of Aunt Liz herself until the August evening she and Julia stepped off the plane into the fierce Florida heat. August was not the time of year to go to Florida. Julia's mother had declined to come for that reason. The night Kathy had won the finals at the Newton Country Club tournament, she had been invited over the telephone by Caroline Collins herself to replace Alicia deLong as one of five New England girls to be represented at the National Championships in Boca Raton, which began two days after Newton. Unable quite to believe this honor which had fallen so suddenly at her feet, Kathy had told Julia, and Julia had told her mother, and her mother had immediately telephoned Aunt Liz, who lived smack in the middle of Boca Raton's Gold Coast. It had been arranged in two minutes' time that Kathy would stay with Aunt Liz, whose house was but a stone's throw from the tournament, and that Julia would go along for the fun. Julia's mother advised Julia that her cousins, Roger and Jeffrey, were two innocent young boys, unaware of northern ways, and that she should not say anything shocking in front of them. "They're nineteen and seventeen, Mother," said Julia in exasperation. "It doesn't matter if they're forty and forty-three," Mrs. Redmond had said right back. "Don't drink, and don't you dare sit in either of their laps like you did when you were twelve."

"Yes, Mother."

"And don't you girls go ordering a drink on the plane."

"Yes, Mother. Mother?"

"What?"

"Aren't you going to tell Kathy to keep out of Roger and Jeffrey's laps?"

"Katherine has far better manners than you, Julia. Katherine is a young lady. I do not ever worry about Katherine. I worry about you."

At Logan Airport Oliver looked for a moment as if he were going to kiss Kathy good-bye. Then he thought better of it, stood back like a soldier who had broken ranks, and waved instead. Kathy, her precious rackets under one arm, waved until she could see no one behind the glare of the morning sun. She waved again through the tiny window of the plane, although she knew her family and Oliver could no longer see her. The plane, the first Kathy had been on in her life, shot down the runway and lifted into the air. She was not so much struck with the extraordinary mechanical miracle of this happening as she was transported, suddenly, with the certainty that this was the beginning of something new, and she was no more in control of the something new than she was of the huge machine which carried her as a helpless passenger. Julia ordered a glass of wine for each of them. The stewardess, wary of their ages, seemed disinclined to bring them until she spotted Kathy's several rackets lying on the extra seat and for some reason changed her mind. The wine swallowed in one gulp, Kathy felt both expansive and groggy. "I feel funny," she admitted to Julia.

"Good funny or bad funny?" Julia asked, knowing better than to guzzle her glass of wine.

"I feel as if I'm sort of in a room all alone."

"You shouldn't drink so fast."

"My folks have to go to Springfield today. They have to move my grandmother to a new nursing home. Dedham . . . " Kathy's voice trailed off. She didn't want to say to Julia that the home in Dedham was cheaper. This even her parents had not easily admitted. Kathy would not have known particularly that this was a fact but for Jody. Jody's remarks, both rueful and triumphant, made it clear that she, Jody, knew more than Kathy and that it was her duty, so to speak, to keep Kathy's feet grounded on the earth by reminding her of her shortcomings. "We can't afford to keep Grandma in the Springfield home anymore" was all Jody had to say to release in Kathy a jerk of guilt, for Kathy knew her tennis had cost several thousand dollars so far and that the better she did, according to hushed late-night squabbles between her parents, the more it would cost in the future.

Kathy closed her eyes against the vibration of the plane and the nausea the wine produced in her gullet. "Rotten luck," Marty had told her the day before. It was Marty's sharp view that Kathy's first air fare should not coincide so closely with her grandmother's being moved. "Don't put those two things together in your head," Marty had warned. "They have nothing to do with each other. You don't understand now, but someday you will." Understanding this logic was beyond Kathy, as Marty had guessed. Since she had been invited to the tournament Kathy had not looked at a magazine or newspaper for fear of coming upon advertisements that included Florida air fares. *Well, I'm here*, Kathy told herself. She avoided Julia's conversation by pretending to stare out the window. She wanted no questions about nursing homes. She had never told Julia very much about her grandmother. The contrast between their respective grandmothers was too great, and nursing homes were part of the no-man's-land between her family and Julia's. The plane passed through a cloud, leaving tiny droplets on the thick window. Then it struck the light, and Kathy found herself staring directly down at a mass of still, white clouds that sat broodingly over the tip of Long Island. *Like looking down at heaven*, she thought suddenly. *No sign of Ruth.*

Had it not been for the "turn of events," as her mother called it, Kathy knew she might not be in this plane at this moment. She might never have won the Newton championship. Mrs. Collins of the New England Lawn Tennis Association might never have made that wonderful telephone call inviting Kathy to Florida.

Kathy could still not reconcile the facts that Ruth had been a superb, strong swimmer and yet had drowned. Mornings, lying in bed, Kathy had constructed a vivid half-dream. She tried again and again to twist the outcome of Ruth's dive. Always the large body in the blue tank suit slipped powerfully into the pool and swam uneventfully to the other side. Then Kathy would open her eyes and know that this was not true. Had there been a puddle on the tiles in which she had skidded? Had she dived clumsily and swallowed too much water, or wrenched a muscle doing that exhaustive butterfly stroke? No one would ever know.

"Why are your folks moving your grandmother?" came Julia's question, too quickly for Kathy. It alarmed her like the sharp surprise ringing of the fire bell during a study hall.

"I don't know," she answered quickly. "I guess it's a nicer place, and Dedham is closer to Plymouth and all."

"You look sad, Kathy."

"I do?"

"Why don't you have your grandmother live at home instead? I've read that even the ritziest nursing homes make the inmates feel like dogs sent off to the pound to die."

"She needs a lot of medical care," Kathy answered. The shrieking of the plane's engines seemed suddenly to come from inside herself, a near-human sound.

"But surely you could get a nurse. . . . "

"Julia! That would cost about three hundred bucks a week, for crying out loud!" Kathy snapped without intending to snap or release this information.

"I'm sorry," Julia said. "That was an awful thing to say. My parents couldn't afford it either," she added in a loyal voice.

"Don't say lies! They could so. Look at your grandmother. She had a nurse for six months before she died, not to mention a maid and gardener."

"Kathy, I'm sorry. Please don't be angry."

"Forget it," said Kathy shortly. *Why*, she asked herself, *am I doing this to Julia just when I need her most?*

"I can't forget it. I hurt your feelings, and I'm sorry. I feel awful."

"Don't feel awful. Just please don't ever look down your nose at me again."

"I *wasn't*. I was trying to make you feel better, and I said the wrong thing. You never, never told me anything about your grandmother before, except she was in a beautiful place with big green lawns around it."

"Well, she isn't. Anymore."

"Kathy, please. Money doesn't matter. It doesn't matter a bit."

"That's a good one," Kathy answered. She was aware of the onset of another headache. It began at the base of her neck and spread as if it had fingers extending to her temples. She tried to look out the window again but was only reminded that the window seat was hers because Julia had been on so many planes before it didn't matter to her to see out. "Money means absolutely nothing to me," said Julia. "I hate people with money. That's why Daddy didn't want me to go to a private school with all the little rich girls and their expensive birthday parties and their own ponies."

"Julia, you just don't understand," said Kathy, and she turned to find Julia crying in the most silent and dignified way she had ever seen anyone cry. She felt as confused as she would have had Julia suddenly fallen and begun to spit blood.

"I remember something," said Julia after she had drawn a settling breath. "The first time I went over to your house, I think it was. When we were both six. In the hall on the shelf were two boxes. One was labeled SHOE MONEY, KATHY and the other SHOE MONEY, JODY. When my mother came to pick me up, the boxes had been taken away. I wouldn't have thought anything, except I asked my mother what shoe money was, and she told me never to mention such a thing to you or your mother or I would hurt your family in some way. Another time I remember having dinner at your house. Jody was about four, and she said it was the first steak you'd had since Christmas. Your mother gave her a look that could have killed a horse. I felt so ashamed of myself for being different. I never thought *you* were different. I used to go to bed at night wishing we were poor."

"Julia, that is the most ridiculous thing I've ever heard in my life."

"It's true."

"Well, if it's true," said Kathy, rubbing the back of her neck, "it's stupid. It's the dumbest thing I've ever heard."

"You feel humiliated, and you want to humiliate me back. I don't blame you at all," Julia added, "but I wish you knew how little money matters to me. Maybe if you win really big, Kathy, and get going like the streak of lightning everybody says you are, you'll turn pro in a couple of years. When you start making scads of money like Tracy Austin or somebody, you'll realize how pitifully little it means."

"When I pay off a few bills, maybe."

"Bills?" Julia asked.

Kathy sighed loudly. "My father and mother combined make just enough to get by," she began, biting off the ends of her words. "With Bobby's doctor bills, which come to about seven hundred since January, and the mortgage and paying off the car loan and my father's new Rolleiflex, not to mention Grandma and not to mention my tennis, we're about three thousand behind. They make what amounts to peanuts, both of them put together."

"They do?"

"Julia, I bet you don't have the faintest idea how much your family has. I bet your folks have never had a fight about money in their lives."

"No. They don't fight at all, really. Sometimes I wish they would."

"Oh. You think that'd be a lot of fun too? Like being poor?"

"I didn't say that. I meant only that it isn't as easy as you seem to think. . . ."

"Not easy? Not easy having somebody else cook meals and wash the dishes every night? Not easy living in a house big enough for ten people? Not easy going to Spain for a Christmas vacation?" Julia was silent. *Was this all coming out,* Kathy asked herself, *because she'd had a glass of wine?* "Do you think I *like* the idea—my folks *like* the idea of putting my mother's mother in a nursing home? Don't you think I *know* it's like putting her away in an ASPCA shelter? Have you ever been in a nursing home?"

"No," said Julia in a tiny voice.

"The smell alone is enough to make you throw up. That and the noises the old people make. The food—all brown and gunky and predigested. The skin on those old people. My God, it's all waxy and white. Even the Black people look gray."

Again Julia was silent.

The sea spun by far beneath Kathy's window, shining like a fish skin, smooth as an egg. Julia's half-full wine glass vibrated in the elastic pocket of the seat in front of her.

"Some people," Julia said at last, "act as if I stole—as if my family went out and stole the money they happen to have. You know who those kids are, Kathy. Now you've got the same chip on your shoulder. Now there is a terrible thing between us."

"Nothing is there between us that wasn't there all

along," Kathy answered, still staring out the window.

"Well, maybe, but I never meant to hurt you. It's what you mean to do that counts."

Kathy thought this statement did not ring true. After all, she had never meant to deplete her family's savings by being good at tennis. Nevertheless, this was happening. It was a fact of life. "It's okay," she answered in a dull voice.

"No, it's not," said Julia. "Don't say it's okay if it isn't. I know I'm going to sound stupid, Kathy—just like my mother when she tries to sound like *Gone with the Wind* or *Wuthering Heights*, but I wouldn't hurt you for anything in the world. I see I have. I apologize from the bottom of my heart. Kathy, you're my best friend in the whole world, and I love you dearly."

The plane lurched slightly. A stewardess walking down the aisle did not seem aware of it. She bounced along, smiling frostily. Kathy tensed against her seat and pulled her belt tight. She shut her eyes against the stewardess's inquiring glance. *How like my mother's that smile is*, Kathy thought. *Cold and condensed. I hope I never smile like that.* For Kathy to show her feelings just now was not in her to do. Julia was waiting anxiously for some reply, but Kathy might have been at the very bottom of the ocean looking up at a distant green daylight and afraid of the bends if she shot to the surface. "It's my fault," she said at last. "I'm mad at Jody for giving me a hard time, and I feel guilty about Grandma, and I'm scared to death about this tournament."

Julia relaxed and finished her wine. "But you'll do so well. You know you'll do well," she said.

Kathy smiled a little. Her head still pounded. "To know I *can* beat everybody there is professional," she answered. "To know that I *will* is hack."

"Now who's looking down whose nose?" Julia asked, laughing.

And Kathy laughed at herself. "Ah . . . you always know when I'm quoting Marty, don't you?" she said.

"Always," said Julia. "Just as you know when I'm quoting Irene Beaufort Redmond." And laughing still, she beckoned in just her mother's manner to the pert, frosty stewardess and ordered another glass of wine for each of them.

If anyone could be more disposed to hugs and kisses than Julia's mother, it was Julia's mother's sister, Aunt Liz. Between hugs Aunt Liz admonished Julia for not visiting often enough, for not living in the South, for having a Yankee Daddy. Then she kissed and hugged Kathy and said it was thrilling to have a famous tennis player as their house guest. Kathy protested that she was not at all famous, but Aunt Liz said, "Fiddle de dee. You will be soon." Then she asked Kathy to call her Aunt Liz, a thing Kathy did with no trouble, as she was unsure of Aunt Liz's last name.

Neither was she sure if it was Jeffrey or Roger who answered the call to drive her to the Hazard Bay Racket Club for evening practice. Whichever he was, he only said, "We'll take my car," and so they climbed into a Jaguar slightly older than Aunt Liz's Jaguar. The brothers, as Julia had said, did indeed look very much alike, and they were both very attractive. Jeffrey/Roger told

Kathy he was going to be a clerk to a judge, or was it a page in the state senate? Kathy couldn't quite make out what he was saying. He wore only a pair of old-fashioned, baggy navy blue bathing trunks. He steered the car with one finger. A toothpick twirled in the corner of his mouth, and in his light blue eyes, which were fixed on the road ahead, was an expression of continual amusement. He did not seem to think Kathy was a famous tennis player as did his mother, nor was he the least bit curious about her or anything she might be doing. In his company Kathy felt quite out of her depth. If Julia's parents had real money, then Aunt Liz had even more of it. She wore a gold choker under the collar of her golf shirt, her license plates read LIZ-1, and she paid someone to clip the hedges around her house into the shape of large birds. At least Kathy guessed they were birds, but she didn't dare ask Jeffrey/Roger for fear of sounding dumb. The expression of perpetual amusement in Jeffrey/Roger's face also frightened her, and she was relieved to jump out of the car at the entrance gates to the Hazard Bay Racket Club.

Before she strode down the main path to get a copy of the draw and to search out a practice partner, to join the girls and boys who were walking around as if they all knew one another very well, Kathy fingered a wall shyly, hoping not to be noticed. The wall was covered with red hibiscus blossoms and looked as if it might crumble at a touch. Coral and adobe suggested themselves to Kathy as she leaned up against the wall's rough surface. A lizard scooted down it and disappeared into a vine, causing her to jump in surprise. The hot air hung here as it did in overheated train cars with sealed windows from which there was no exit. Flowers seemed to grow without benefit of earth, on walls, in crevices, in piles of what appeared to be crumbled shells. Would a strange flower take root on her hand if she were to sleep outside all night? Were there poisonous snakes? Did the coconuts fall from the tall palms and hit people on the head during matches? She pictured herself being hit by a coconut as she was about to serve, but this only reminded her sharply of Ruth.

According to Oliver, the day Ruth had died, people at the Plymouth Club had talked of little else. The day after that their interest trailed off, as there was little to discuss, and then life had continued in a perfect string as it had done before. Time closed up over Ruth's existence as the high tides closed up twice a day over the jetty, leaving no trace of the rocks. There had been a day or two when people felt squeamish about using the pool. First the children, who didn't know or understand, had gone in, then the adults, who knew better than to be queasy, and at last all the teen-agers. Since almost no one had ever noticed anything about Ruth or her family, she was, as Kathy saw it, like a dead letter.

Kathy walked straight through the unfamiliar Hazard Bay Racket Club grounds and found the beach. While jogging her two miles down the sand she also found a Californian to practice with whose name she instantly forgot.

As many as sixty times in a row Kathy and the girl from California slammed a ball back and forth across the net in the heavy dusk. There was still, for Kathy, an exquisite wonder to this ritual. It drained her of worries and of sadness. In this simple near-dance with a stranger she was consumed with joy in the execution of every perfect stroke. Her happiness, unfettered as a very young child's, mounted until she was lost in it, grinning at her nameless partner, who grinned back from across the net.

No scores were posted, no tricks contemplated. The girl was an excellent player. *What a thing it is*, Kathy thought, *to be happy about that and not try to beat her*. She was aware that she loved the game best when hitting without hatred and without calculation. She also knew that this was not supposed to be so and that it was a pity she felt that way because that feeling would likely trip her up someday, as Marty had warned. Nonetheless, as the other girl returned a particularly difficult backhand with a yelp of pure ecstasy and Kathy returned that shot low and hard to exactly the same spot, catching the girl out of position and causing her to laugh out loud at herself, Kathy supposed that this exhilaration and unity with another person was found seldom, except by people in lifeboats and catchers on trapezes.

"Come," said the California girl. "Come meet some of the kids. There's a welcoming party tonight in the main clubhouse. Food and everything. Are you staying with a family or in the motel?"

Kathy followed the girl uneasily. She did not want to meet the kids. On the one hand she was frightened of so many strangers all of whom seemed to know each other. On the other hand she didn't want to appear a silly, frightened loner. "Who's your first round tomorrow?" the girl asked. Kathy answered the unfamiliar name, stumbling over it.

"Oh, ho!" said the California girl. "Lucky you. You know she's only ten? Playing up."

"No, I've never heard of her."

"Couple of issues back *Tennis World* did a piece on her and a bunch of other babies. She's on the cover. I know her. She comes from Santa Monica. I think you can take her though. Keep away from her backhand. It's like a cannon. Most of the kids hate her. She's spoiled. Cries all the time when she loses. Little brat. Clothes all custom made with her initials on the collar. Copied straight from Tinley designs . . . " The girl turned and fixed her friendly slanted hazel eyes on Kathy's dress. "Yours are made by hand too, though, aren't they?" she asked.

"My mother . . . likes to sew," Kathy answered, feeling herself blush. Kathy owned six wash-and-wear tennis outfits made from store-bought patterns by her mother. The dresses fit her well and were quite pretty; however Kathy longed for a Bogner tennis dress or even a pleated heavy linen Fred Perry skirt. Those things were unaffordable by her family, and there was simply no chance of having them. It was enough that she wore out a pair of twenty-five-dollar sneakers every three weeks. As Kathy and the California girl neared the clubhouse she noticed the clothes of the other players who sauntered around. Each one looked like a model for one or another maker's outfits. Suddenly she hated her plain white dress with the red and white gingham facing. The party would be twice as unnerving since Kathy felt as conspicuous as if she were dressed in black.

"We'll shower," said the girl. "Then we'll go have a beer. I know some kids who've sneaked in a case of Coors."

"No, thank you," said Kathy, suddenly stopping short of the clubhouse. "I'm expecting a ride. It's late. I have to wait out by the gate."

"Well, see you around," said the girl and waved.

A pair of high French doors opened into the central clubhouse, revealing to Kathy what lay inside. There was a fountain with revolving colored spotlights and four marble cupids. At the bottom of it coins winked and glittered. Lost wishes for tournaments past? There was a junior boys' tournament going on somewhere nearby, and so the room was filled with boys and girls. They stood and talked in groups, not in a way, Kathy decided, she had ever stood in a group but in the easy way grownups did. Near the fountain stood a girl Kathy recognized immediately from pictures in tennis magazines. Johnson or Jackson was her name, nationally ranked about sixth in fourteen and under. A Black girl from Detroit, or was it Cleveland? She seemed to be looking for someone. Another highly ranked player, or another Black player? Kathy wondered, it never occurring to her that the girl might feel as lonely as she, because she was not only a good player but as beautiful and poised as a full-grown woman.

Kathy, keep your mouth closed when you smile, your braces reflect. Kathy, you walk like a boy, said her hygiene teacher's voice in her head, and silently Kathy stepped backward and walked away down the driveway, the crumbling stucco wall at her side under her fingertips. She reached the outer gates and stood by them in the shadow of a thick, squat palm until Jeffrey/Roger should come back for her.

Aunt Liz herself came for Kathy. Because Kathy could think of nothing else to say, she asked Aunt Liz to tell her the bullet story, which Aunt Liz was delighted to do, stretching the details out until the moment she pulled into the driveway and turned off the ignition, the air-conditioner, and the stereo, which had played some un-enduring Broadway show tunes the whole of the trip.

Dinner was served by a butler, whose name Kathy did not catch, on the terrace beside the pool. The presence of Jeffrey and Roger, whom she could not yet tell apart, the butler, and Aunt Liz came between Kathy and Julia, and Julia seemed more a part of them than Kathy wished. Aunt Liz sat low in her leather-padded wrought-iron chair. Kathy's eyes took in the whole of her, although she tried not to stare, and not to gobble all those unidentifiable things on her plate that lay under various sauces.

There was, to begin with, Aunt Liz's turquoise-blue silk blouse and the deeply suntanned face, nearly as dark as a new penny. The gold choker had been replaced by pearls. In her conversation Aunt Liz made easy reference to past events and people, all unknown to Kathy but all apparently extremely important or amusing. This served to make Kathy feel desperately ignorant, and she looked across to Julia for support, but Julia's eyes did not catch hers. Aunt Liz's right hand bore two diamond rings, and it held **and** set down a wine glass without allowing the glass to make a circle on the tablecloth as Kathy's glass had done six times so far. Each of Aunt Liz's fingernails was a perfect oval containing a perfect white moon, and her hair moved in the slight breeze as if it had been orchestrated just so.

Kathy wondered how such a woman could ever have thrown a vase at Julia's mother, since she was positive Aunt Liz was not the type ever to be angry, dirty, or even to go to the bathroom very often, if at all. A brief argument occurred about whether Kathy's telephone call home should be made collect, which Kathy lost. As she excused herself to make the call Aunt Liz remarked that she was sorry to have forgotten to have steak that night but that she hoped it would not affect Kathy's match the next day. It was Aunt Liz's view that athletes ate only large amounts of steak and raw eggs.

The telephone rang ten times before Kathy remembered that her family was probably somewhere between Dedham and Plymouth, possibly still at the new nursing home with her grandmother. Evidently it had been a long day's work. She could see Bobby's head resting in Jody's lap in a waiting room somewhere. The lounge at the Springfield home had been pleasant enough with comfortable overstuffed chairs and fresh flowers in crystal vases. Would this second home be all that much worse? Would it be dirty and dreary with plastic armless furniture like the bus-station waiting room in Boston? She remembered the salmon-colored plastic lounges there. They had stuck to the backs of her thighs one hot night.

"Marty!" said Kathy aloud before she dialed Marty's number, as if to assure herself that she was going to call Marty. Her fingernail caught slightly in a beige silk sofa cushion, causing a run in the material. Kathy turned the pillow over and placed it at the far end of the sofa. As she dialed the number she had written on the side of her sneaker in case she lost it she stared straight into the face of an Inca dancer that had been assembled out of copper and brass pieces and stuck to the wall opposite her. He was very large and expressionless with only a suggestion of a face, as the metal bits, like small wings and shelves, were meant to be an abstract design. Kathy told Marty about the ten-year-old whose picture had been on the cover of *Tennis World*.

"You know who she is, don't you?" Marty asked.

"No."

"Kathy, with one of the most famous last names in California tennis?"

"Oh, gee, I didn't know there was another sister," said Kathy.

"Well, there is, and she's it, and you can take her," said Marty, "even if she has been coached for nine and a half years and has played against her older sisters and brother, not to mention her old man, who's the biggest coach in southern California. Keep in mind, she's only ten. She won't have much of a serve yet, so don't hang back too much. She'll have a fast return herself, since her brother and sisters will have served to her as hard

as they can. I know these young superstar types. She'll
have learned to cover the whole court, so this is what you
do. Are you listening?"

"Yes, Marty."

"Don't give her what she's used to. Don't play a base
line game. She'll wait for you to make an error in a long
rally. Spin your serves, even your first serves. Dink her
and lob her and get her off balance. Act like you're having a ball doing it, smile, and you'll drive her crazy and
have her where you want her, mad as a hornet. Remember one thing."

"Yes, Marty."

"She won't have much court sense yet, she's too inex-
perienced. You have to play really mean to get court
sense, and her sisters won't have played that mean.
Watch for signals. Since her father is her coach, he won't
do anything, but her mother may signal from the stands.
She can't stop herself. You'll recognize her because she
looks like Judy Garland after a bad night. If you see the
little angel looking up at her mother or see a hand raised
or anything, call the referee. Only if you're sure. She'll
lose her concentration after that. Remember, little Miss
Muffet's old man has put about forty grand into each of
his kids, and this one's a spoiled brat. You play fair but
mean and make her feel ten years old. It'll mess up her
game, and she's got it coming. Who's your second
round?"

"Either the seventh seed or a girl named Foster from
New Jersey."

"It'll be the seed. Where's she from?"

"Port Washington."

"Well, don't let her ranking bother you. Just be a little hungrier and a little better than Miss Port Washington. She's probably loaded. Most of those kids are. You know Angie McKenzie, the sixteen-year-old whiz at Wimbledon this year? She's a Port Washington special too. Her last tournament she was playing one of the older pros. Someone in her thirties. Anyway, McKenzie started off the match with a rally of a hundred and thirty shots from the base line before one of them netted a ball. She completely exhausted the other player. Nearly gave her a heat stroke. I want you to know what some of the girls do. There's no way you can lose to this girl if you use your head and play your own game. Don't get mad and don't get scared. Remember that dummy who almost beat you at Quincy . . ."

"Marty, please. The girl drowned . . ."

"That hardly makes her a saint, my dear, or a good player. Just keep certain things in the forefront of your decent little Christian mind. Tennis is full of smarties like Angie McKenzie who'll do anything to win. You have a reputation preceding you for blowing your stack, and I want that reputation killed right now in this tournament. If you get a bad call, stare straight ahead. If you double fault three times, follow it up with three aces. I want you to go into every match as cool as ice inside. You do that, and Miss Port Washington is going to think a snake bit her after the first set. Do you understand me?"

"Yes, Marty."

"Tell me what you understand."

"I've got to control my temper."

"If you do, you'll be a leg up on every opponent. Believe me they'll all have a couple of notes about your famous thin skin. They'll try to get to you. Make it a waste of time. Did you do your two miles?"

"Yup, and it's about a hundred and ninety degrees here."

"Don't eat much breakfast. Go into both matches knowing you're going to egg both girls. Just remember they've both had every advantage that you haven't. Their parents are rolling. They have private courts at home. Private lessons at the age of four. Girls like that are trained like racehorses. Born with a silver spoon, Kathy, full of caviar. Grandma puts a grand in the savings bank every birthday, and they leave a gut-strung racket out in the rain and Daddy buys them another one. Are you there?"

"Yes, Marty. I'm listening."

"Good. Call me tomorrow night same time. I know people down there. They'll be watching you."

Kathy said good-bye and rubbed her ear as if Marty's words were still lodged in it. Trying her own number again, she gazed at Aunt Liz's living room as the distant telephone rang unanswered. She definitely could not recall ever having been in a room as clean as this in all her fourteen years of being in various rooms. She hung up the telephone and, checking to make sure she was unobserved, stepped cautiously around, going first to the copper and brass Indian, or so he seemed to be. She looked closely at the gleaming pieces of metal and decided that if such a thing were to be in her own living room, she would have placed tiny objects on each of the shelflike precipices. Perhaps pebbles or coins. The pure white carpet was as soft as down and as deep as the second knuckle on her finger. This was not a room in which a somersault had ever been turned, a dog had ever lifted a leg, or a piece of pizza had landed cheese side down—*And you'd better get out of it before anything happens,* Kathy advised herself. She opened the sliding glass door and between two whispering palms stepped out into the night.

Once she had seen a photograph of a night sky as luminescent as this one. In a *National Geographic* some years back she had pored over a picture of the Taj Mahal at midnight. Behind the minarets lay a deep indigo heaven as cloudless and star ridden as this. *How must it be,* Kathy wondered, *to come down to this place straight out of a Massachusetts February? How must it feel to stand in this warmth with your feet still cold from the Logan Airport parking lot?* Julia's family flew down to Florida frequently in the wintertime, as Mrs. Redmond complained that the New England dampness got into her bone marrow. Julia came too, missing school, and as it didn't affect her grades, the teachers didn't mind. Julia, Kathy reminded herself, was also born with a silver spoon and as a child had left any amount of things out in the rain, and these things had been replaced without too much fuss. There had been a bicycle which rusted after two weeks behind the lilac bush. Then there was a doll. Kathy had never seen the doll, but Julia's mother was fond of telling the doll story. At four years of age Julia had been given a French porcelain doll by this very Aunt Liz. It had real hair and a silk brocade ball gown. Julia had forgotten it one day and left it on the grass, where it was ruined by a northeaster; it was found in the woods a week later, crushed by a fallen tree. Julia was to be punished for this, "and we really tried," Mrs. Redmond had said with a resigned chuckle, "but she refused to sleep for a week without it, and when she went on a hunger strike, we had to get her another." Julia claimed not to remember the event, but Kathy guessed it was true since Mrs. Redmond told the story often without changing the details.

Kathy took one more glance through the glass into the living room where she'd felt so ill at ease. In this house, in the Taj Mahal itself, she decided, Julia would probably scorn the furniture just as she did at home. In the Blue Room of the White House she would sit with her back on the floor and her legs propped up against some priceless antique chair. Her presence anywhere would be as inviolable as the greenness of leaves or the drumming of raindrops.

Long after Kathy had gone to bed, she opened her eyes on a yet sleepless night. She listened to the pounding surf outside and to Julia's regular breathing on the other side of the room, wishing the two rhythms would coincide exactly. *Think only about tennis*, she repeated to herself, trying to re-create the sound of Marty's voice, or her mother's. *Don't start another argument with Jody. Don't think about Grandma. Stop picturing Oliver when you caught him in the shower. Stop picturing Ruth not drowning*. She changed position for what seemed to be the thousandth time that night. The sheets were soft and slithery under her. *If I win it all, and never stop,* Kathy reckoned, *I'll have everything someday. One pro tournament championship with a big check, and I can pay back every cent my lessons and sneakers and everything else has cost. One pro tournament, and I'll never sleep on those awful muslin sheets that Mother cuts in half when they get holes and sews up again with that uncomfortable seam.* At last the sound of the ocean breaking on the beach caught up with her thinking, and she slept. It seemed after a minute that her eyes had opened again, this time on the inside of her head.

What she saw was one of the three dwarves that stood in the front yard of their neighbors' house. He had been there as long as Kathy could remember, although she did not know the reason why the people next door had chosen such things to be in their front yard. Upon him the snow had fallen and the November leaves. Summer sun had bleached his red hat pink. Against him Kathy had occasionally tossed a stone, and so his body was chipped. The dream had occurred to her several times recently. In it Kathy found herself to be in deep terror of this dwarf, although he did not move; she ran from him because under his quaint gnome's hat were Dutch boy bangs.

"Mommy, Mommy!" she heard herself cry out but in a deeper voice than her own and in a pitch so desperate it might have come from a woman who had been suddenly shot.

"Kathy, what's wrong? What's the matter?" Julia was shaking her out of the dream.

"What?"

The bedside lamp was switched on. "Kathy, you're dreaming. Wake up! It's okay. I'm here. You're down here in Florida with me and Aunt Liz. You're okay!"

Kathy blinked in the light. She felt Julia's hands firmly holding her shoulders, and she felt herself gag. She pushed Julia aside and made her way to the bathroom.

When she returned, an astonished Julia was still sitting on the bed. "Is it the heat?" Julia asked. "I don't understand why they have August tournaments in Florida of all places. They must be crazy. I'd die of the heat."

"Southern kids play outdoors all summer," said Kathy, shaking her head. "They can't just place the Nationals in Maine every year, you know." The sight of Julia in her familiar pink forget-me-not nightgown was comforting, and Kathy managed a weak smile. "Sorry," she said, "it's like this before every tournament." She tried but could not remember the dream.

"You never told me that! You mean you get sick before every match?"

"Usually in the morning. I never wanted to tell you," Kathy added.

"But that's awful, Kathy. I never imagined it was so hard for you. It looks so easy when you play."

Kathy shrugged. "A lot of the girls have it worse than me," she said. "You know super number-one Jennifer Robbins? The one with the hundred-mile-an-hour serve and the big boobs?"

"You've mentioned her."

"She told me, one day when we were waiting out a thunderstorm, she not only gets sick before every big match, but her whole insides turn to water. She goes out and murders all her opponents anyway, so it doesn't matter. She eats nothing but rice and boiled steak the day before, but it doesn't help. She just tries to find a ladies' room away from everybody else."

Julia winced visibly at this description. "I'd quit tennis if that happened to me," she said.

"No, you wouldn't," said Kathy, smiling a little more. "Even you'd lose your sense of modesty after a while. No one cares, really. We've all heard a hundred girls get sick or cry or sit moaning in a chair all doubled up with cramps. In a few months you wouldn't even notice."

"Are you still angry at me?" Julia asked suddenly.

Immediately Kathy switched out the light and got back into bed. "No," she said. After a moment had passed in which she listened once more to the insects and the ocean, she added, "You know how I am."

"How?"

"Well, I'm not too Yankee, as you always say, for some things. I get terribly mad when I play badly, and I swear and cry. I guess I'm not too Yankee to come to you whenever I'm upset, but . . . I'm too Yankee, I guess, to be able to put things into words the way you do. To say I'm sorry . . . or much of anything."

"I know," said Julia kindly. "It's okay."

"It's funny. I hate admitting things like this, but this evening over at the Hazard Bay Racket Club I wouldn't go in and meet anyone. I was scared of them, and I waited out by the entrance for half an hour rather than face all those in-group looking kids. The whole time I waited, I felt like the world's biggest chicken. I wish you'd been there, Julia."

"Kathy?"

"What?"

"Someday soon you're going to be a better player than anyone at that silly club tonight, and you're going to start believing in yourself."

Kathy won both her matches the following day. The famous ten-year-old she dispensed with in twelve games, and the seventh seed from Port Washington in sixteen games. She felt a twinge of pity for the ten-year-old, who looked to be only eight. She was a thin girl with flaxen pony tails, almost colorless blue eyes, and a French tennis outfit that would cost at least a hundred dollars in most pro shops. In the locker room after the match she sat in a hard wooden chair and sobbed as if she had been suddenly orphaned. Kathy knew the girl was probably afraid to face her mother, because she'd seen the mother's face just before the match point was served. Kathy did not identify the woman's features, having no idea what Judy Garland looked like after a bad night, but she could single out that rigid, dark expression, the set of the jaw, and the eyes, as offended as a chained dog's. Kathy hoped the girl had at least a teddy bear and that it wouldn't be taken away.

The other girl, Kathy's second-round opponent, simply disappeared after the match. She had thrown her racket to the ground and not retrieved it. These incidents Kathy reported to both her mother and Marty that night on the telephone to their satisfaction.

What she did not tell her mother was that Aunt Liz had observed that Kathy had every right to look just as snazzy as the rest of the girls and had taken her down to the local tennis boutique and advised her to choose three or four new outfits. Kathy did not mind this slight to her mother's tailoring or her family's income quite as much as she hankered after a real Bogner tennis dress. Although they cost over seventy dollars apiece, Aunt Liz paid for all three as casually as she would have paid for three Cokes.

Perhaps the dresses brought her the unimagined luck, for Kathy won and won until she reached the finals, where she lost to a girl whose picture had appeared in *Sports Illustrated*. By that time she had been interviewed by a local Florida paper and by a *Boston Globe* reporter and had received a congratulatory telegram from Kenneth B. Hammer of the Plymouth public schools. This she threw away, as it made her uneasy.

Up the ocean drive toward the Plymouth Club Kathy pedaled in the rain. She tried to avoid the muddy splashes of oncoming cars and trucks, but she could not, and in a short while she was drenched to the skin, just as Julia's mother had said she would be. She didn't mind. It was a great relief to be away from the stifling Florida air, and there was a jumpiness inside of her that could only be lessened by jogging or pedaling. Since the club was too far from Julia's house to be jogged to, she had borrowed a bicycle, and ignoring Mrs. Redmond's insistence on driving her, she was on her way. It occurred to her that her success in Florida had at least for the moment shot her past the age when someone else's mother could absolutely forbid her to do something.

In Kathy's pocket was a clipping Mrs. Redmond had saved from that morning's *Globe*. The clipping had been flapping in Mrs. Redmond's outstretched hand when she met Kathy and Julia at Logan Airport that morning. "Kathy," she had explained breathlessly and protectively, "your mom and dad are tied up. Your mom's with your grandma and your dad has to do a photography thing for the VFW, so you come right home with us, but, oh, Kathy, look at this! Read what they said about you in the morning paper! Julia, I want you to read what the *Boston Globe* has to say about your best friend."

Kathy pulled to the side of the road to let a moving van pass. She patted the article with her free hand. It was still dry, folded in a tiny square and stuck in her bra. Would Marty have seen it yet? Of course. Would she be truly pleased? Yes, but would she say so? Probably not. *She'll ask me what the girl beat me with in the finals,* Kathy decided. *And I'll have to go over that rotten drop shot all week.*

In the finals Kathy had faced a girl of just the sort Marty and her mother loved to hate. She was ranked fourth nationally. She had lustrous long dark hair, heavy eye makeup that did not run, and a solid gold necklace that shone against her deeply tan skin. The girl had been written up in *Sports Illustrated.* At home, which was in Houston, she had a private clay court and two coaches, one who appeared every morning at six thirty. The girl had not beaten Kathy easily. Kathy didn't care a bit that she'd lost to her. She was so delighted to have come as far as the finals she had smiled broadly after the match point, something she guessed she oughtn't to have done, and the girl from Houston had congratulated her with grace and affection, as if Kathy had won.

Would her mother and father have seen the papers yet? Kathy hoped so. It might make her mother's vigil at her birdlike grandmother's bedside a little more bearable. For Jody, of course, it would do nothing. Jody started an argument in Kathy's mind beginning with *You were spending two weeks playing in the sunshine while all the rest of us were in a foul-smelling nursing home . . .* When Kathy had last seen her, her grandmother had been temporarily attached to a beige machine. The machine hummed and then stopped and then hummed again. Kathy had been told its purpose but had deliberately forgotten what it was for.

"Dear God," Kathy muttered, "please make Mom and Dad happy and untired tonight and please make Marty happy and please, please make Jody shut up for once." The wind and rain blew furiously against her, and Kathy knew that these things were not God's business. Rose, the Redmonds' Rose, seemed to know God's business well.

At her welcoming-home/victory-party lunch Mr. Redmond had made a joke about the Boston papers. The headline on her precious clipping read "Hub Girl Wins Big!" Anyone, Mr. Redmond had said, who had ever spent a night in Boston or within a hundred miles of it would rate as a "Hub person" as far as the Boston papers were concerned. There had been lighted candles on the dining room table and a fire in the dining room fireplace, as the day was cool. Kathy had spent several Christmas dinners with Julia's family, and this lunch was very like a

Christmas dinner. The heavy silver service, engraved illegibly with Mr. Redmond's grandmother's initials, created a sense of eternal security as it clanked on the gold-edged plates. So did Mr. Redmond's unsqueaking wing-tipped shoes and his clean strong hands. Kathy's father's hands were equally strong but stained with nicotine and photographic acids. The house and Julia's whole existence were a place of eternal springtime where the dogwood was always just in bloom and only the promise of summer lay ahead. This springtime was magical for Kathy to share but, like a ring behind a jeweler's thick glass window, it was not at all really hers. *Julia, with no adversity or trial to test her, will inherit a diamond mine at the end of the story*, Kathy decided, recalling a children's book. *And me? Ah. Now I remember what's bothering me.*

"Here's to our Kathy," rang Julia's mother's voice in her head. "Honey, you may have lost the last game, but—"

"Match, Mother," Julia had corrected.

"You may have lost the last game," Mrs. Redmond went on, raising her glass of brandy so that it caught the candlelight, "but the important thing is I can see from your happy face that you are able to take both victory and defeat in stride. I remember not long ago you being all het up about losing to some young lady who cheated—"

"My God, Mother," Julia interrupted again. "It doesn't matter Kathy lost in the finals. She lost to one of the best fourteen-year-olds in the whole country! The girl's going to qualify for the U.S. Open. She was a junior Wimbledon quarter finalist. That's not losing. That's winning!"

"Julia," said her mother, "I was toasting Kathy. You will please not interrupt. Kathy has learned something about life which you fail to understand. Last time she was very upset at losing to that awful cheating girl—"

"Mother," said Julia with more than usual heat, "the girl's dead. That was Ruth Gumm. The swimmer at the club."

"I was not aware it was one and the same person," said Mrs. Redmond, lowering her glass without drinking from it.

The mention of Ruth had immediately provoked Rose, who was at that moment serving a floating island. Rose's eyes had brightened, her back stiffened like a cat's when it has heard a mouse, and she had announced that such things were no accident.

"Oh, now, Rose," Mr. Redmond had said, but Kathy had known they would let Rose go on. The only way to shut Rose up, Julia had told her once, was to let her speak her piece. Otherwise she was inclined to sulk and boil the entire next meal.

"Only yesterday," Rose went on, dishing out an extra large portion of floating island to Kathy, "Cora told me about it. The Gumm child, may the Lord have mercy on her, had bad blood in the family. It's been put out that there was foul play."

"Oh, Rose," Mrs. Redmond had said.

"Dear heart," Rose continued, "the family ordered an a-u-t-o-p-s-i-e!"

"Y," said Mr. Redmond.

"The good Lord only knows why she was struck down," said Rose.

"No, Rose. I meant the letter *y*. *Autopsy* is spelled with a *y*," said Mr. Redmond. "And I'm positive there's a regular explanation for it. The girl probably had a cardiac arrest. Such things happen occasionally, even to youngsters. They are just following normal procedures, I'm sure, Rose. It isn't every day a champion swimmer drowns in a pool."

"That's just what I mean," said Rose.

Silly, Kathy told herself now. *Just gossipy old Rose, who, as Mrs. Redmond put it, sees a black widow spider in every cobweb.* "Don't be silly, Rose," said Mrs. Redmond reassuringly in Kathy's mind. "The girl was locked in at the time of the accident. There wasn't a soul around. It was an unfortunate tragedy. This is lovely floating island, Rose. Did you use your mother's recipe?"

Kathy did not mean to ask the question in such a way. She hadn't really meant to ask it at all, but when she had stepped into Marty's office and closed the door on the wildly blowing rain, she felt her whole face light up. "Are you proud of me?" she asked. "Marty, are you proud of me?"

"You did what I knew you could do," said Marty. The *Boston Globe* was open before her.

"Oh, Marty. If I won the women's final at Wimbledon next year, would you be proud of me then?"

Marty looked up from the paper. "One thing at a time, my dear," she said. "You did brilliantly. You know that. You know perfectly well what I think. You'll do even better now that you've gone this far. You have the New England Championships this weekend in Newport.

You should win the whole thing. It'll put you on the map. Now what did this Texan Jewish American princess beat you with?"

"Drop shot to my backhand a hundred times. I was way out of position. But she had it all over me, Marty. She must have aced me a hundred times too." Kathy sighed and glared purposely up at Marty's bulletin board. She noticed suddenly that it was bare. Even the photograph of Marty beating Maureen Connolly was gone. The trophy case was empty, and in the corner where the stacks of ball cans and unstrung rackets were usually piled, there was nothing.

"I may be taking a vacation for a couple of weeks," said Marty, following Kathy's eyes with her own. "We can work on the public courts. I've checked with Joe Potter over there, and it's fine with him."

"What? How can we work anywhere if you're going on vacation, Marty? You never go on vacation," said Kathy.

"I want you to keep up your momentum. There will be a lot of tough players against you next weekend, my dear. You won't even have an easy first round."

"Marty, what's happening? Why is all your stuff gone? You're not even in tennis whites."

"It's raining," said Marty, fixing her eyes on Kathy's. She wore a baggy old tweed skirt and a gray cable-knit pullover. Kathy realized that she had never once seen Marty out of tennis whites, and she felt a shock, as if suddenly all the oxygen had been sucked out of the air. The rain clattered on the shingles outside and dripped in splayed torrents from a tin drainpipe near the door. Marty squinted at a leak which had formed under the windowsill. "It won't work, you know," she said, as if this were part of an ongoing discussion. "Fred Molina's being an ass, as usual. He's trying to get me fired. He wants Gordon to come in here as the pro, and do you know why? Because Gordon married that little Italian snip. They all stick together like tent caterpillars. It won't work. Fred and I never got along, but I didn't think he'd stoop this low."

"How can he have you fired? What grounds does he have? He can't just up and have you fired, Marty!"

"Trumped-up grounds, my dear. The most vile pack of lies I've ever heard. Nastiness and scandal, and it needn't concern you. Now. I want to hear every detail of every match you played down in Florida. What is that foolish expression on your face?"

"It's nothing, Marty. Well, just that my dad's people came from Italy a hundred years back or so. They changed the spelling of their name from—"

"Don't be ridiculous. You stayed with Julia Redmond's family down there?"

"Yes. It was lovely. It was amazing. Her aunt went out and bought me three Bogner dresses. I don't know what to do with them. I'm afraid my mom might get mad because she spent nights making my real dresses. I mean my—"

"Oh, she won't get mad because of that," said Marty. "She'll get mad because she'll think you were goldbricking off Julia's aunt. A silly idea. I don't believe in looking gift horses in the mouth. Give them to me. I'll have them dry-cleaned. Then you can tell your mother the company sent them to you free."

"But that's a lie, Marty."

"Your first, my dear?" Marty asked, her head cocked to the side and her eyes as bright as a terrier's.

Kathy shook her head and looked at the floor. "Marty," she asked, "how can Mr. Molina have you fired for just nothing? It isn't fair."

"Life is unfair, my dear. You should know that better than anyone."

"Why me?"

Marty paused a moment and rolled the cuffs of her sweater up. "Because," she said slowly, "if it hadn't been for that unfortunate accident a couple of weeks ago, you might never have won the tournament at Newton. You wouldn't have been invited to Florida, and you might not be on your way to the New England Championships this weekend, would you? Life was not very fair with that stupid lumberjack of a girl who kept beating you the whole week you hit with her. You had very good luck, my dear, and she had very bad luck."

Unable to answer, Kathy imagined a shadow person had looked in at the window and for a second focused piercing eyes on her from a face obscured by fog. "Do you really want to know?" Marty went on. "I'll tell you. That stupid puff-breasted old grandmother Molina said that I tracked up his precious pool house. That's it. Tracked up his pool house with tennis court clay. They dislike me, my dear, because of my nasty personality. They dislike me because I won't take any guff from the lazy fatheaded children of the local mucky-mucks who are forced to take lessons from me. Because I won't kiss the hands of their martini-soaked card-playing Mamas who sit in their cabanas all day polishing their nails and reading the smut on the best-seller list. That's why. Because I'm not very nice, Kathy, as you know well. If I had ten geniuses on my string at this club, I could pull them all out at a moment's notice, and the management would think twice about losing ten family memberships, but I only have one, Kathy, and your family doesn't even pay, so I'll have to wait it out."

"I'll resign in protest, Marty."

"How can you resign if you don't really belong? Not only that, my dear, you have to work as a lifeguard for your bread and butter. Don't sneer at money. As a matter of fact, if this is not cleared up by next week, after your tournament, you may take over some of my lessons. You can beat any man in the club, and you're good enough to teach the kids. You can use some extra money. I know about your grandmother. I know your family has tried to keep the money part away from you and that your sister rubs all the salt she can in that wound."

"Marty, I couldn't. You need the money too."

"Be smart. Don't be stupid. In three years, I assure you, you'll be able to pay me back with interest. Now tell me about Florida."

"First tell me why they are firing you."

Marty looked out the window again. "It's letting up," she said. "Go do a mile in the wet sand. It's worth two miles in dry sand."

Kathy trudged out to the beach. She took off her already sopping sneakers and socks. "Plymouth's rising star—a fierce ball of fire with a shotgun serve, reminiscent of a young Rosie Casals"; that's what the *Boston*

Globe had to say about her that morning, but the words did not make her as happy as they had before. They sounded like a Jordan Marsh ad.

The waves curled, filled with pebbles and ugly brown seaweed. They flew seven feet in the air before smashing on the broad gray beach and sucking themselves back again. Many years before there had been a northeaster such as this. Kathy recalled that she and Julia had collected hundreds of seahorses that had come north in the current and had washed onto the beach. Another time there had been sand dollars and translucent gold shells which they were sure they could sell for a great deal of money. This day there was nothing washed up but stones and a few waterlogged, splintery beams, as if the furious ocean, foaming at its mouth, was trying to fling them at her as she ran down the beach, only missing by a bit. On her return she spotted Oliver's lonely figure watching her from half a mile away.

Kathy stood in the middle of the living room. She held her arms above her head in a gesture of triumph that she had observed in the movie *Rocky*. "Guess what!" she crowed when her father came downstairs to greet her.

"Guess what? I've seen the papers!" he also crowed happily. Kathy's mother beamed from the kitchen like a living lightbulb. Everything was in confusion for a few moments as Kathy was battered with questions about Florida, about her opponents, about Aunt Liz's house. "But guess what!" she finally managed to say again. Her mother dried her hands on her apron. "What could be better, Kathy?" she asked. "What did you do? You met

Billie Jean King and hit with her and beat her love and love?"

"No, Mom. I just won five bucks from Oliver."

"Doing what?" asked her mother.

"Oliver, you tell," said Kathy. "They won't believe me."

"Kathy can really positively throw to first base as accurately and as fast as Rick Burleson," said Oliver solemnly.

"Who's he?" asked Jody. "By the way, congrats for creaming 'em down there," she said blandly, turning to Kathy.

"The Red Sox third baseman, that's who," Oliver explained. "This afternoon when the rain cleared up, the baseball field was empty. So I put Kathy on third and an apple basket on first base. Then I hit her a bunch of tough grounders. She threw to first and got the basket every time, and I timed her with a stopwatch. Last week I timed Burleson's throws in a game and averaged out the exact times. Kathy did it. Only one second more than Burleson."

Kathy's mother had lost interest in these facts and announced from the kitchen that there was nothing to eat but TV dinners so they might as well go out to Burger King and celebrate Kathy's victory.

"It's okay, Mom. I had a big lunch at the Redmonds'. Roast beef and the works. I'd rather stay home."

"And lobster and salmon and crepes suzette?" Jody asked.

"Kathy's wasting her time in tennis," said Oliver. "She's only one among many women. In baseball she could be the first and only woman."

"Oliver," said Kathy's mother, placing the TV dinners in the microwave oven and stepping back from it in case it exuded harmful rays. "Get out of the way," she said to Bobby. "You never know. Oliver, Kathy is not going to be a baseball player, and that's that. Sit down everybody. This only takes a minute."

"Think of the endorsements," said Oliver, undaunted. "Kathy's picture on everything from fielders' mitts to Alka-Seltzer."

"I wouldn't do that if I won the U.S. Open," said Kathy.

"Don't look down your nose yet," said her mother. "You know how much Willie Mays makes for advertising Brut? You know how much Bancroft pays Billie Jean for that ad?"

"Let's not get ahead of ourselves," said Kathy's father. "First things first. Shall we tell her?" he asked as he opened the foil over his dinner and let out the steam.

Her mother, her father, and Oliver all wore identical smiles. Only Bobby, who was piercing indentations into his tinfoil with his fork, did not seem to be listening. Then there was Jody, who only stared glumly at her gray Salisbury steak. "Wait," said Kathy. "Don't tell me. Let Jody tell me."

"Why should I tell you?" Jody asked, tossing her hair out of her face.

Because I'll get it straight from you, was what Kathy wanted to say, but she didn't. "Because," was Kathy's answer.

Almost gratefully Jody put down her fork. Like a professor about to list the causes of the Civil War, she leaned forward and said, "If you win your next tournament, they're going to change your coach, or at least get you some famous one part-time. You're going down to some clinic, they call it, in Florida for an eight-week eight-hour-a-day crash session or else down to Port Washington, New York, to this other guy whose name I forget. He sounds like a kangaroo."

"Harry Hopman?" Kathy asked in astonishment.

"Yes!" shouted her mother. "And—"

"I'm not finished," said Jody.

"Eat your dinner," said her father.

"How can I eat this stuff?" Jody asked. "This meat was frozen in Kansas City seven years ago. And also, when school's in session, they're talking about taking you down to Newport, Rhode Island, every day to this other guy. Mom has to take off more time from the shop, and I have to baby-sit—"

"Jody, eat. That's enough," said her mother.

"But what about Marty?" Kathy asked.

"You may have learned all Marty has to teach you, honey," her mother explained smoothly. "This happens to everyone who really is tops sooner or later. Kathy, a man like Hopman is your ticket to the national circuit. You know that. He's coached McEnroe, all the big young players. It's like . . . like Daddy buying a Rolls-Royce instead of a Ford."

Kathy watched Jody's face carefully. Jody had opened her mouth, and then she snapped it shut as, unaccountably, her mother held up one finger and said, "We don't want to talk about what happened Sunday, do we?"

"I don't really care if we do," said Jody.

"What happened Sunday? Why is everybody in on everything except me?" Kathy asked, looking from one person to another.

"Nothing happened," said her father.

"I punched a nurse in the kisser," said Jody.

"You may leave the table," her mother announced.

Kathy's father watched as Jody left. He seemed satisfied when the kitchen door closed, and giving Kathy his attention, he leaned on his folded hands and explained, "Kathy, in three days you have the New England Championships. It's the biggest deal so far, now that you won in Florida, of your whole life up to this point in time. Understand, honey?"

"Yes, Dad."

"Tomorrow you have an algebra exam. Have you forgotten?"

"Yes, Dad," Kathy admitted.

"I thought so. Well, you better crack the books tonight. After that you have nothing to do but run, work out all your kinks on the courts, sleep, and eat. You've got to be ready Saturday morning for the biggest match of your life. Now you've been away for a while, and you have to catch up. Nobody's keeping a thing from you or excluding you."

"I'm going to work out with Marty."

Her father did not respond to this statement. Instead he and her mother and even Oliver began indulging in what Kathy found to be a mortifying amount of speculation about her future, tournaments to come, and what they had read in tennis magazines about life in a clinic in a faraway state.

There had been many nights when Kathy had failed to fall asleep right away, and many afternoons when her attention had wandered from her books, when she'd pictured herself holding up the huge silver cup at the U.S. Open or that big plate at Wimbledon. In these daydreams she always gave a short speech. She changed the speech around every time she gave it in her imagination. She would have been mortally embarrassed to admit to holding up dream cups or thanking Billie Jean King for a bouquet of roses, yet here were her mother and her father and Oliver doing nearly the same thing.

"Got a few well chosen words in mind for when you win the finals next week?" Oliver asked. "They have a microphone, and you'll be on local TV."

"Come on, Oliver, you'll jinx me."

"Hopman's the best coach in the country," said her father, going on with his conversation. "Hands down. No one can touch him."

"Van derMeer," countered Kathy's mother, blowing on her coffee.

"Okay, but he spends a lot of time with middle-aged hacks."

"He worked with Heldman. He worked with King."

"Are you excited, honey?" her father asked, as if he had just remembered that Kathy was there. "Do you understand the full meaning of this? Do you understand the full meaning of what you did down in Florida?"

"It means she has to do it again," came Jody's disembodied voice from the den.

"Go to your room, Jody," said her father sharply. "If you aren't big enough to share a little of your sister's happiness, we don't want any glum faces around the dinner table."

Kathy looked down at her plate. Slowly she spooned some gray gravy into an indentation in her mashed potatoes. "I don't want to leave Marty," she said. "Not as a regular coach, anyway. Why is Marty being fired, Mom? Does it have anything to do with this stuff about getting me a new coach?"

"Kathy, eat your potatoes. Of course not," said her mother. "Sooner or later you're going to have to go to a top pro and hit exclusively with other top players or your game won't progress. You know that. Eat your mashed potatoes."

"Well, just tell me why she's being fired or suspended or whatever is happening."

"Kathy, you know perfectly well Marty has a hot temper. She got into a fight with the club manager, and it's all Greek to me, but that was bound to happen too. Marty just isn't very popular, and unpopular people don't last. Eat your potatoes."

"They taste like old . . . forgotten oatmeal. Why was she fired?"

"Oh, my!" said her mother. "We *are* getting expensive tastes, aren't we? How about the silverware? That's not as good as the Redmonds' either, is it? How about some baked Alaska for dessert?"

"Mom, I'm sorry. I know you've been in Dedham all day. I'm just not hungry."

"Honey," said her father kindly, "if I get some Kentucky Fried Chicken, will you eat it? It's your favorite. You've got to eat."

Kathy took a careful forkful of potatoes and swallowed it. "I'm working out with Marty," she said as defiantly as she dared. Her father signaled something down the table to her mother that she did not catch.

"Okay," he agreed. "But no more baseball. Oliver, you hear that? She can pop a shoulder out making like Rick Burleson."

Kathy let the conversation go on between her mother and her father while Oliver cleaned up the kitchen and carried Bobby upstairs for his bath. "Are you listening, honey?" her mother asked once, and Kathy nodded, but she was not listening. She was not listening until after Oliver left and by chance, on her way to brush her teeth, she caught the tail end of a conversation downstairs. Her foot had creaked on the stair landing, and she would not have paused had her mother's voice not stopped suddenly.

"Jody knows everything," her father had been saying.

"Shush!" her mother had answered sharply. "Later. When the children are asleep!"

Kathy brushed her teeth more noisily than usual.

"Night, Mom. Night, Dad," she called, and as they said good night and told her to sleep well and long she closed the door to her room, still standing in the hall.

Three years earlier, when she and Julia had experimented with cigarettes in her mother and father's bedroom, which already smelled of smoke, Kathy had memorized the squeaks of every board in the floor of the upstairs hall. "Jody," she whispered after she had crept down the hallway like a thief and had sat softly on Jody's bed so as not to alarm her. "Jody!" She placed a hand on Jody's bare shoulder.

"I knew you'd come," whispered Jody. "I'm awake."

"Jody, what's happening around here? First of all, why are you in trouble? What's this about socking a nurse?"

Jody punched her pillows against the headboard and sat up against them. "I lost my temper," she whispered loudly.

"Shush!" said Kathy.

"I lost my temper," she said again in a smaller voice. "I noticed, by the way, that nobody mentioned poor Grandma. Everybody was too excited about you, including you."

"I was going to ask," Kathy faltered, "but . . ."

"Nobody wants to disturb a nice TV dinner with unpleasant details, do they?"

Kathy put her face in her hands. "You don't understand," she said. "I was going to, but I was afraid . . ." Here she began to cry and shake so that she stopped talking. When she'd regained a little anger, she asked, "*Why*, Jody? Why are you always, always so mean to me? Don't you know you make me feel like a piece . . . worse than that. You make me feel like some evil person who ought to be electrocuted or hung or something."

Jody did not apologize. She toyed with her top sheet and rubbed the material over one finger and against another. At last she said, "Hey! Cut it out. You want to know what happened?"

"*Yes!*"

"Sunday afternoon?"

"For starts."

"Well, I really didn't punch the nurse. I just sort of slapped at her."

"A nurse! Why?"

Jody sighed. "You know what they're doing to Grandma in this new place?"

"God, no."

"Well, they have these little pills on her bed table. I asked the nurse what they were for. I mean I know she needs medication, and I was just interested. I wanted to know because . . . I like to know about those things and all. Anyway. The nurse said one was a sleeping pill and one was a laxative. I said, 'How come they're prescribed for every night?' The nurse said it was the policy of that place to give all the patients sleeping pills and laxatives because it made it easier for the staff to get them to sleep and to clean them up all at one time. Well, she didn't actually put it that way, but that's what it amounted to. Anyhow, I told that dirty, lousy Nazi nurse that that was a fine way to get Grandma dependent, addicted to those pills. That it was just dandy for the staff but not so dandy for Grandma and that they hadn't put her in diapers in the last home. You know they used to take her to the john when she wanted? So I took the pills and tossed them out the window. The nurse had a fit! She grabbed me by the shoulder, and I told her to get her grubby Spanish Inquisition paws off me. Then she grabbed me by the other shoulder, and I just let her have it. I only gave her a little tap, but the stupid idiot cut her lip on her tooth, and you'd think she'd never seen the sight of blood in her life. You know Mrs. Finn's cat that used to howl all night? She sounded just like that. Anyway, by that time Mom and Dad came in, and the nurse called the supervisor, and the security guards rushed in when they heard all the noise. The nurse wanted to file an assault-and-battery charge, but Dad smoothed it over." The fire went out of Jody's eyes. "I just wished one thing," she added, playing with the edge of the sheet again.

"What, Jody?"

"I just wished . . . I loved Grandma so much when she was alive . . . I mean when she was normal and younger and when she lived here with us. We used to laugh all the time at the silliest things. I even said a little prayer that though she can't talk much or recognize people, somehow God had kind of opened a window in her mind, in her brain, for just those few minutes and that she heard me. That somehow she knows I still love her and that she was laughing at the nurse too and that she wouldn't think we had just abandoned her."

"Good for you, Jody. Good for you!" Kathy whispered. She wished she could reach out and hug her sister, but she thought it might embarrass Jody if she did. Particularly if Jody was still angry. "I would have done the same thing," Kathy asserted strongly.

"Would you?" Jody asked.

"You know my temper."

"I've seen it on the tennis court . . ." Jody's sentence trailed off in thought.

"I would *so* have done it," Kathy insisted. She waited for some approval from Jody, but of course it didn't come. A chilly wind blew the curtains aside, and Kathy shivered. "Jody, I would have hit her. I probably would have taken out two teeth and landed myself in the can," said Kathy, trying to laugh a little.

"Okay. Okay, I believe you," said Jody. "Now I'm going to sleep. Good night."

"Not until you tell me the rest," said Kathy.

"What rest?"

"What's going on, Jody? What's this about Marty and this new coach business?"

"Just what I told you. They're sort of applying to these famous coaches like applying to a college."

"Jody, what happened with Marty?"

"I don't know anything about it."

"Jody, you're a lousy liar."

"Kathy, I made a promise. I don't break my word."

"Come on, Jody, I'm your sister. It affects me directly. If you think for one minute I'm going to sit there and cheerfully pass my algebra final and cheerfully concentrate on tennis, you're wrong."

"Kathy, I gave my *word*."

"You know what?"

"What?"

"On the plane home from Florida I was talking to Penny Snider? Well, her little brother was going to be a ball boy at the Newport tournament this weekend, but he has to have his adenoids taken out, so there's an opening. You want me to tell Mom? I'm sure she'd love to have you pick up a few bucks being ball girl for seven straight days."

"Kathy, you wouldn't."

"I would so. Unless you tell me everything you know."

Jody considered. "Only if you make me two promises."

"What promises?"

"First you promise not to say I opened my mouth."

"Of *course*."

"Second you have to answer one question and swear to God that He may strike you paralyzed from the neck down if you lie even one little bit."

"Okay."

"God, I hate to break my word," Jody muttered.

"Oh, Miss Saint," said Kathy. "Miss Holy Mother of God. Jody, you know just how to get under my skin. I know I'm not the best person in the world. I know I have faults, but you don't have to lord it over me all the time. How would you feel if . . . if one day you sat down at the piano and started to play symphonies out of your head, and everyone went crazy and started spending money on lessons and pianos for you? And I gave you a lot of gas about how la-di-da you were and was jealous and mean? How would you feel?"

"Okay, Kathy. You win. But you made two promises."

"I know. I know."

"Well, let me begin at the beginning. Marty's being fired or suspended. She was interviewed by the police."

"The cops! Why?"

"Well, what happened is this. Apparently after Ruth Gumm drowned, her parents, Ruth's parents, had an autopsy done. They thought she might have had an undetected heart condition or something. The report came back that she drowned all right, but the whole lining of her lungs was seared. They—"

"Seared! Burned?"

"Irritated. To make a long story short, they think somebody poured about a hundred times too much chlorine in the pool the night before. Ruth dived in and swallowed some, and I guess she choked and threw up and drowned. The cops said it was probably meant as a prank. No, not exactly a prank but that someone wanted to either make her sick or more likely affect her vision temporarily. Nobody intended to kill her of course, but you know what chlorine does to your eyes. Ruth used to swim without goggles. Everybody does because it's a salt-water pool and they don't use much chlorine because the water's always fresh from the ocean. Anyhow, they found the traces of chlorine in her. Of course the pool was drained right afterward, so they couldn't check the water, but they're sure."

"But what does this have to do with Marty?"

"Well, Mr. Molina was cleaning out the pool house that morning, and he found a footprint, a sneaker print, and he cleaned it up, not thinking anything. But when the news came out about the chlorine, he showed the sponge to the cops. They have the clay sample from Molina."

"But it could have been anyone. Why Marty?"

"Kathy, it wasn't green clay from the club courts. It was red clay. The only courts around with red clay are at Newton, and Marty was at Newton the day before Ruth died."

"But . . . but so was I, Jody. And you for that matter, and Oliver and Mom."

"That's right, Kathy."

"But, Jody. But . . ."

"The cops called Molina right away. They interviewed Marty right there in his office."

"How do you know all this?"

"You know the Malones' dressing room? Number one eighty-four? It's right over Molina's office. You could drop a dime through the floorboards onto his desk. Anyway, Peachy heard the whole thing. I bribed her with free ice cream from the snack bar. As much as she wants for the rest of the summer. She listened to the whole thing and told me. Marty's in trouble, Kathy. She won't say where she was the night before Ruth drowned. Says it's her business. She got really mad at Molina apparently and told him he had a fat rear end and connections with the Mafia, right in front of an Italian police chief! Marty's crazy."

"But, Jody, they can't prove anything. So what if they have a little bit of red clay? They don't have an actual footprint. Even if they did, so what?"

"Kathy."

"What?"

"Ruth's mother is making a big deal out of this. Somebody apparently tried to harm her daughter and wound up accidentally killing her."

"Somebody."

"Yeah. Somebody, Kathy. Now you keep your end of the promise."

"Okay. Shoot," said Kathy.

"First you swear."

"How?"

"Put your hand on my hand. Okay. Now, do you swear to tell the truth, the whole truth, and nothing but the truth so help you God, and if you lie, may God strike you paralyzed from the neck down?"

"I swear."

"Okay," said Jody, releasing Kathy's hand from a tight grip. "You remember that night before you were supposed to play Ruth at Newton? Bobby got sick, remember?"

"Yes."

"And Mom had to go to Norwood for the prescription, and Daddy took Bobby to the clinic, and Oliver had to leave early to help with the club party?"

"Yes."

"Where did you go?"

"I went to algebra like I always do . . . and practice. I went down to the public courts."

Jody's eyes burned. She sat upright suddenly and held up her hand as if she were about to hit Kathy in the face. "You dirty rotten liar," she said. "You *deserve* to be paralyzed! Don't you remember? You left without any books. I covered for you. Mrs. Diggins called up and asked where you were, and I said you were off with Daddy. That it was an emergency. I figured you just went straight to the courts to work on your serve. Then I remembered. You didn't take your racket. Now where were you, Kathy?"

"Jody, I swear up and down I didn't go near that pool. I didn't dump any chlorine into anything. I swear!"

"Where *were* you then?"

"Why do you have to know? Why can't you just believe that I didn't have anything to do with it?"

"You know why? Because somebody might start asking questions, that's why. Because somebody's kid got killed, Kathy, even if it was by mistake, and it might have been over a tennis game. A *tennis game*. You had a lot to lose if Ruth beat you."

"Oh, Jody, I know, I know."

"Where did you go, Kathy?"

Kathy looked out the window for a moment. The rain had begun again, and it was spitting in over the sill. She got up and closed it. "Fenway," she said. "I took the express ball park bus. The Yanks were playing the Sox."

Jody began to laugh a little. "You idiot," she said kindly. "I believe you." Her teeth had started to chatter. She hugged Kathy hard and added. "I hope you have a ticket stub or something."

"I thought you believed me."

"Oh, Kathy," Jody said, and shook her head. "Forget it. Never mind."

/ 7 /

Kenneth B. Hammer was a very likable man. His feet were large in their splendid brown loafers with the gold buckles. His hands were warm and dry, and his large hamlike thighs strained at the seams of his pants. His hair was a warm brown and brush cut, like a marine's. "I hear you're quite a little ballplayer," he said to Kathy with a toothy grin worthy of a master politician.

"Yes, sir," Kathy answered. She waited for him to stop shaking her hand. When he did, she sat opposite him in an uncomfortable old student's desk, the only other place in the principal's office to sit. She thought Mr. Hammer looked as uncomfortable as she behind the principal's dignified mahogany desk. Evidently this was so, because he leaned back in the equally dignified mahogany chair and, clasping his big hands behind his head, propped his feet on the radiator.

"I mean, apart from your tennis," he went on. "You did terrific down in Florida, honey, by the way. We're all real proud of you. You went into that situation and showed the stuff a champion is made of. But what I mean is I hear you're some kind of shortstop too."

"Oh, well," said Kathy, feeling herself redden. "I guess I play a halfway decent shortstop."

"Used to play a little semipro myself," said Mr. Hammer, and he picked up a round glass paperweight containing a preserved rose and made as if to pitch it across the room. "Boy, I'd like to be your age again, honey," he said. "What an unbelievable situation you're in. Young, pretty, and loaded with talent. You know everybody around here thinks you're going to go all the way?"

"Thank you," said Kathy, wondering when he was going to hand over the dreaded algebra exam. "I'll do my best."

"Sure you will. You've got all the tools, but more important, the right attitude. So you like baseball too?"

The sunlight poured in directly behind Mr. Hammer's head. Kathy could not see his expression well except for the continuing grin.

"I love baseball. But I'm a girl, and I'm too small and . . ."

"Too bad about the Sox this year."

"Yes . . ."

"You play with this fellow, what's his name, a lot?"

"You mean Oliver?"

"English. That's the one. Little fellow. Seems like he

thinks you've got a great arm. Thinks you can throw like a pro."

Kathy shifted around in her one-armed seat. "I don't know really, Mr. Hammer," she said. "Oliver is always timing people with stopwatches. He makes up little tests for me. Yesterday I won five dollars on a bet from him because I threw to first almost as fast as Rick Burleson two times out of three."

"It's great, honey, but don't do too much of that. You could tear a rotator cuff. Your arm's your bread and butter." Mr. Hammer stood and passed Kathy the examination papers.

"Hope it doesn't upset your boyfriend if you quit baseball," he said.

"Oliver's not my boyfriend," said Kathy. "He's just my friend."

"Sure," said Mr. Hammer. "Nice boy though. Works hard. Know anything about his people?"

Kathy frowned. Something was wrong here. Why was she sweating? "No. I guess his folks are divorced and all, and he lives with an uncle."

"Poor kid. Had a rough life," said Mr. Hammer. He rocked back and forth on his heels, his hands in his pockets tightly. Kathy noticed that Mr. Hammer's loafers creaked. "Seems to have straightened himself out nicely, though."

"Oliver?" Kathy asked. "Straightened himself out?"

"Got in a peck of trouble when he was about eleven. Put big upholsterers' tacks under his stepfather's tires. Guy got a flat, a blowout, and nearly went off a bridge. Tried to have the kid charged on delinquency and all that, but the kid was too young. Never did anything after that."

A warning light blinked in the back of Kathy's mind, or so she felt. "I know all about it, Mr. Hammer," she said as coldly as she dared. "Oliver told me about it the first night I met him. His stepfather was an addicted gambler and gambled away his mother's hard-earned money and drank himself silly every night, also on his mother's money, and I told Oliver I thought he was morally right to do it."

Mr. Hammer smiled and tapped Kathy's paper with his fingernails. "Do the best you can on this thing, honey," he said with a comfortable chuckle. "I had old battle-ax Diggins when I was your age. She gave me a D-plus, as I remember, and whacked me once a day! Just leave it on the desk and let yourself out when you're through. Go out the side entrance. The main entrance is locked."

Mr. Hammer was gone. The room seemed actually larger without him. The sunlight hit her paper directly. Kathy squinted at it and smelled the mimeograph fluid in the purple print. To Kathy each of the neatly typed and numbered problems might have been a mile of thread, gnarled and knotted for hours by some maniacal baby. Above her a clock ticked in a blond oak frame. Every time its big hand advanced, it jumped slightly. On the top-most shelf of the oak bookcases beside her a bust of Lincoln stared down at her, blindly but judgmentally. Kathy squirmed. On the corner of the principal's desk lay the Algebra I textbook. She wondered if Mr. Hammer had left it there to test her honesty or to allow her help during the exam. She gazed at it for one long yearning minute by the clock, then hunched herself up over the first problem. "A freight train," she read aloud in a blandly reasonable singsong, "leaves station A for station B at two P.M. It is traveling at twenty miles per hour. The distance between stations is ten miles. Another freight train"—Kathy repeated this for emphasis—"*another* freight train leaves station B for station A, also at two P.M. It is traveling at ten miles per hour." She wrote down 10 and underlined it. "At what time will the trains pass?" She drew an A and a B and connected them with a line filled in with tiny crosshatches representing ties on a track. After drawing both trains with smoke coming out of their stacks, she said, "Easy! At what time will they pass? Let x equal one train. Let y equal the other. Let z equal two P.M." It doesn't mention separate tracks, she thought. They'd crash! She decided to let this first problem sit for the moment.

The next one concerned itself with a transaction between two butchers. The third had to do with bridge spans and the fourth with a tire's revolutions per minute.

Kathy was bathed in sunlight and in sweat. The open window allowed the sound of a tractor and the smell of newly mown grass to waft through the office. *Do they expect me to cheat? Is this a trap?* she wondered miserably as her attention switched once more to the book on the edge of the desk. In it lay the answers to all the questions on the test. Somehow Kathy's memory was good enough to recall the trains and the tires and the two butchers because she always pictured them as in life when given a problem, and she knew practically to the page where she would find her answers. The butchers she'd pored over earlier that summer in Mrs. Diggins's house, mentally making one Black and one Chinese to keep them separate as x and y. Motes of dust settled softly on the blue and orange cover of the book. *I will not cheat!* Kathy told herself, gripping her pencil tightly. *You already did the first time around,* said another voice. *I will not cheat. I'm better than they think I am,* she said to the book on the desk. *Not at algebra, you're not,* said the same logical voice.

The textbook seemed to her a center of evil. Its temptations throbbed at her like an unstoppable Latin rhythm section. Kathy got up from her cramped desk. She took the large flat textbook in her right hand, and eyeing the top of the bookcase, where only a ladder could reach, she threw the book as accurately as she could and shouted, "Get out of my sight!" and called it a vile name.

It was one thing to throw the book fifteen feet in the air but quite another to get it to land flat on a shelf. After trying twice more and having the book land both times at her feet, temptingly open, Kathy succeeded in angling it right. It lay forever out of harm's way but had ricocheted off the bust of Lincoln, which had split in two as it landed on the principal's desk.

"You stupid dope! You dummy!" Kathy yelled at herself. "Now look what you've done!" Desperately she rummaged through all the drawers in the desk hoping to find some glue, paste, anything that would repair the damage. The drawers were empty save for paper clips and erasers. "Dummy," she said again. "The bust's probably an antique worth five hundred bucks." Sweating and dirty from the dust she had raised, Kathy began to weep softly. She took the two sides of the bust and held them together. The break was clean and the sides held. She put Lincoln on a low shelf and tiptoed back to her desk.

I've done the right thing with the book, she assured herself as she looked at the fourth problem. "If the speed of a wheel must be increased by thirty percent to reach a speed of thirty revolutions per minute," she read in a shaky monotone, "what is the original speed of the wheel?" Kathy drew thirty circles, each to represent one revolution. "Increased by thirty percent . . ." she muttered. She drew a hundred more circles as quickly as she could. "Okay, a hundred circles equal a hundred percent. Therefore thirty circles equal thirty precent. Add that to the other thirty circles and you have your answer." Kathy wrote 60 in the answer box. *It can't be*, she thought. *Sixty is either a hundred percent more or fifty percent more, I'm not sure, but it sure isn't thirty percent more.* She swore out loud and banged the soft end of her pencil against the desk. On the shelf the bust fell open quietly.

Miserably she looked from the bust of Lincoln to the description of two butchers who were exchanging a hundred pound side of beef worth two hundred dollars for a seventy pound side of pork worth sixty-five dollars and eighty cents. *Soap* she thought. *I'll stick it together with soap.*

In the girls' room, which Mr. Hammer had thoughtfully unlocked for her, Kathy found each of the glass soap dispensers empty and cleaned, ready to be filled for the coming year. She nearly cried in happiness when the last of them turned out to contain a white residue in its bottom. Kathy pumped at it, all the while sweating as much as in any match in the broiling sun. She could neither pump the soap out nor unscrew the globe, *but it's better to have a broken soap dish than a broken bust of Lincoln*, she reasoned, and she cracked it open with a plastic toilet brush she found in the corner.

Kathy scooped out the dry soap and placed it in a little mound at the side of the sink. She carefully worked it with warm water until it attained a gluey consistency. "Just like real paste!" she told herself in her encouraging algebra-problem voice. Some of it she used to repair the handle of the toilet brush, some to repair the glass globe, and the rest she carried back into the principal's office in a paper towel and lovingly applied it to the inside surfaces of Lincoln's head. It held nicely this time, with hardly the appearance of a crack. *It should last all year*, Kathy told herself, *if nobody bumps it or lifts it*.

But what if the principal tries to put it back on the top shelf? Kathy asked herself as she sat down again. *What if it is an expensive antique? I can't just say it fell down. Mrs. Diggins'll be sure to find the book up there, and she'll know it was me who took the exam in this office, and then I might even get Mr. Hammer into trouble if she finds out he was going to let me cheat!* Kathy was certain of one thing. She could do no more algebra with her imagination so rampantly on the loose. *I must solve this calmly and sensibly*, she decided. *All I have to do is get Lincoln back up there and the book back down.*

Between the shelves and the window, behind the American flag, was a thin heating pipe. She thought she could shinny up it using one foot for balance on each bookshelf. But not holding a heavy, fragile lump of plaster of paris. But she *could* wrap the head in something carefully and hold it in her teeth for just those few seconds it took to climb. The only piece of cloth available save her shirt or shorts was the flag. *I know Mr. Hammer will come in if I take off my shirt. I know it,* she told herself, and so she removed the flag from its pole easily, as it was only stapled on.

It took her less than a minute to wrap the head and a few seconds more to get her balance and replace it perfectly in the dustless square from which it had fallen. On her way down she retrieved the algebra book.

The clock showed more than an hour and a quarter had passed. *Wasted!* Kathy scolded herself and resignedly looked up the answers to all the problems, allowing herself only a barely passing grade.

She was folding the flag as she had been taught to do in Girl Scouts when Mr. Hammer came back into the office. "I was just folding the flag, Mr. Hammer," said Kathy.

Mr. Hammer peered at the flagpole.

"It came off," Kathy added.

Mr. Hammer offered her a ride home as he slammed the office door and locked it behind them. On the shelf the bust came apart. "Place is falling to pieces," he said sadly, watching it through the glass.

"I have my bicycle, thanks," said Kathy.

Mr. Hammer tapped the pocket of his jacket where he'd placed Kathy's exam. He smiled his big smile and winked at her. "Now you go play your heart out, honey.

By next week you should be the New England champ."

Afterward Kathy wondered if everything would have turned out differently had Mr. Hammer not winked in the sly way he did.

"Mr. Hammer," Kathy asked in just the voice she'd used to say *another* freight train, "could you give me back my test, please? I'm ashamed to say I cheated on it. I'd rather take a failing mark than have that on my conscience . . . please, Mr. Hammer?"

"Now, honey . . . *honey!*" he warned as he straight-armed Kathy away from his pocket. "We're just going to talk about it, okay? Just talk about it first, all right? Now calm down. Settle down. We're going to talk about it. Everything's going to be okay. You're under a lot of strain. I've seen this happen a hundred times in a pressure situation."

"I've seen this happen a hundred times in a pressure situation," said Mr. Hammer confidently to Kathy's father and mother.

"I think the pill is doing her a little good," said her mother. "Kathy, do you feel any better?"

"I feel . . . groggy," Kathy answered. "But no better, Mom."

"That's okay. You get something to eat and you'll feel a hundred percent," said Mr. Hammer.

Kathy blinked at him. He was sitting on the sofa in her living room, holding a drink between his large opened knees. He was smiling. "Quite a little fighter!" he said with a grin. "Now once again, Kathy," he went on in a very warm and easy tone. Kathy watched her mother and father watching Mr. Hammer. What time was it? Evening. "Once again, honey. Two things have to be clear in your mind. One is that you never cheated on a tennis court, did you?"

"No, Mr. Hammer."

"Of course not," echoed her mother. "She doesn't have to."

"That's what counts, isn't it?" Mr. Hammer continued. "You think you cheated on the exam, Kathy, because you're so worked up about the other thing. You've got a good little conscience there. I admire it. But you're all upset. You cracked under too much heat, Kathy, and when people are upset, they do things and say things they don't mean and that they're sorry for afterward. Now trust me, and trust your mom and dad. We're grown-up people, Kathy, with a lot of years behind us. You've only been a kid so far."

Kathy's feet were folded neatly beneath her on her favorite rose-covered chair. Mr. Hammer's logic and his expression were like a thick flawless blanket. Warm and inviting. Impenetrable.

"Now only you know whether you fudged a little bit on the test, but what we all know, Kathy, your mom and dad and I, is that you had an unbelievable amount of pressure on you in Florida. You stood up to it incredibly. You had a lot of pressure today in a subject you hate. You've got a lot of pressure coming in two days with the Newport tournament. Now you add to that a lot of unfounded gossip and a big imagination, you're going to come up with a little breakdown."

"I haven't had a breakdown," said Kathy.

"Nobody takes a tranquilizer unless they've had a breakdown," interrupted her mother.

"Will you please tell me, Mr. Hammer"—Kathy felt her voice rising—"how come you knew all that stuff about Oliver, right down to the kind of tacks he used?"

"Routine, honey. He comes from another town. Moves here for the summer. Police do a routine check. Happens a hundred times a week. I happen to know about it because the police chief, Dom D'Amico, is my wife's brother-in-law. I knew you played ball with the fellow, and I wondered who he was. That's all."

"First you're after Marty. Now it's Oliver, isn't it?"

"Nobody's after anybody, Kathy," he said sadly. "Nobody did anything to anybody. What you've heard is a lot of rumors."

"I will not play," said Kathy. "I won't eat or sleep before Saturday unless everybody stops hiding stuff and comes out with it straight. I'll hear it from you," she added, "or I'll find out for myself."

"She'll hear it from some other dingbat source, Ken," said Kathy's father.

Mr. Hammer leaned back on the sofa. He snapped his fingers softly. "Stubborn as a little mule," he said, whistling between his big white teeth. "Well, that's why she wins the big ones. Okay."

"Please tell me what's happening," Kathy repeated.

"Kathy," her mother broke in, "Ruth Gumm's parents are trying to stir up a hornet's nest."

Mr. Hammer took over again, seeming to have decided what approach he would use. It was the friendly one. "*Hornet's nest* isn't the word for it," he said, catching Kathy's eyes with his own. "Kathy, I want you to listen hard now, okay? Just relax that active little brain of yours and listen. Please?"

"Okay."

"First of all, these people— Don't get me wrong. They lost their kid. They're very, very upset about it. I understand just how they feel. But they didn't go to the police, Kathy."

"They didn't?"

"No. They went straight to the head of the New England Lawn Tennis Association. Caroline Collins. *She* went to the police. Now again, maybe they weren't thinking straight. Their daughter had a terrible accident. But it was an *accident*, Kathy. A terrible tragedy. But that doesn't give them the right to pin it on someone else. To lay blame and try to find a scapegoat, does it?"

"Well . . . no."

"Do you think it gives them the right to upset many other people's lives just because they're upset?"

"Well . . ." Kathy began.

"You know, honey, sometimes grown-ups can act just like children. When a kid can't accept a disappointment, what does he do? He lays on the floor and has a tantrum. He says, 'My brother did it!' He says *anything* to get around it! Well, in the face of personal loss and tragedy some people, adult people, do the same. Rather than living through a bad situation and facing up to it, letting time heal their wounds, they use up all their energy flying around like a chicken with its head cut off. Blaming, accusing, heedless of the feelings of others, they try and change what they can't change. You know, my wife has a little what-d'ye-call-it, needlepoint thing on the wall of our kitchen. It says 'God grant me the serenity to accept what I can't change, the courage to change what I can change, and the wisdom to know the difference.' That make any sense to you, Kathy?"

"I've seen them. The needlepoint samplers. I know what it means."

"Okay, Kathy, now I'm going to ask *you* a tough question, and I want *you* to give me a truthful answer."

"Yes, Mr. Hammer?"

"You think you're ever, ever in your whole life going to be able to add two and two and two?"

"You mean math?" said Kathy, looking down at her hands.

"I mean math. Do you ever think you'll play the violin in a concert?"

"No," Kathy answered questioningly.

"You ever think you're going to be a great ballerina?"

"No."

"Do you think you'll ever be any good, even good enough to pass first-year algebra, at math?"

"If I studied, maybe."

"Did you spend all last year and all summer studying?"

"Yes, Mr. Hammer."

"Did it do any good? Can you change it, Kathy? Can you change it? Can you learn the violin or ballet or math?"

"No."

"Then accept it."

Kathy was silent.

"Okay?" he asked.

"Okay," she said unsurely.

"Now I'm going to explain something else nobody can change. When Police Chief D'Amico gets charges, when someone charges somebody with wrongdoing, the police have *no choice*, Kathy, but to pursue it. To investigate the charges. It's the law. Now it's my personal opinion that what happened is a terrible misunderstanding, but this is what has come down the pike so far. The cops have a specimen of red clay that the club manager wiped up off the pool-house floor. The pool water, at the time of the accident, was overchlorinated. After the autopsy Ruth Gumm's parents went to Mrs. Collins at the NELTA. They thought you or somebody close to you had tried to harm their daughter because she had beaten you many times and was to play you the next day. Mrs. Collins went to the cops, and the cops came to Molina. He was very defensive. Thought they were accusing him of carelessness with his pool. He showed them the sponge with the clay on it and said the tennis pro over there had been messing around in the pool house and it must be her fault. Now it looks to me like your club manager wanted to get your tennis coach fired. He didn't really think there was any funny business. He just wanted to clear his name from a negligence charge. There's a feud going on between the two of them. Doesn't look like the coach is too popular."

"Marty?"

"You like her?"

"Without Marty I'd be nowhere."

"Oh, come now, honey. Marty didn't give you your talent. The good Lord did that."

"I will not leave Marty."

"Okay, okay. But just supposing this Marty person had decided to tip the match in your favor that day. Just supposing."

"Marty would never do that," said Kathy.

"We don't know where she was the evening before. As a matter of fact anybody who spent the day at the Newton Country Club and got their feet full of that red clay could have gone into the pool house. To tell you the truth, D'Amico's been too busy to do much about this yet. We do know where you were, Kathy, thank God."

"She was at algebra and down at the public courts practicing," said Kathy's mother. "Just ask Mrs. Diggins. Ask Joe Potter."

"I was at Fenway Park," said Kathy.

"What?" asked her father in horror. The atmosphere in the room changed so suddenly Kathy became alarmed. "It's okay," she said. "I came home after the fifth inning. I didn't want to be late, and the Yankees were winning anyway."

"Oh, boyoboyoboyoboy," said Mr. Hammer.

"You could have been raped! Mugged!" said her mother.

Mr. Hammer held up his hand for silence as if he were in a disorderly kindergarten. "Can you remember a bus driver, Kathy? Do you have a ticket stub?"

"No, sir."

"Remember someone who sat next to you? Anything at all? Anybody see you? A guard? Did you talk to anybody?"

"No, sir."

Again Mr. Hammer snapped his fingers softly and distractedly rubbed at his jaw. "Listen, listen, listen," he said. "Kathy, we've got a completely wrong slant on this. There's no homicide charge here. It was an accident no matter how you slice it. Nobody wanted to kill the poor girl. Even if what her parents say is true, that somebody did dump some chlorine in the pool, it was at worst a practical joke. Do you understand that?"

"She died," said Kathy.

"She died of drowning, Kathy. Not of chlorine. Chlorine can't kill anybody. She could have died in the ocean swallowing too much salt water if the salt water made her gag and closed up her throat and she couldn't breathe. That happened to me once, snorkling off Jamaica. If I hadn't been close to the boat and two fellows hadn't dragged me out of the water, I would have drowned just because I swallowed too much salt water and it came up and I couldn't control the spasm."

"People don't die of practical jokes," said Kathy.

"Honey, a four-year-old wouldn't try to *kill* somebody by putting chlorine in the water. No, no, no. *If* it was intentional, honey, somebody only meant to incapacitate the girl's vision, or maybe her sinuses, very slightly, and our only concern here is the New England Lawn Tennis Association and whether they suspend you from the Newport tournament. Not the police, Kathy, the NELTA!"

"Well, what *are* we going to do about the NELTA?" Kathy's mother asked suddenly. "What *are* we going to do if they suspend Kathy from the tournament Saturday."

"I'm not playing anyway," said Kathy. "I'm giving up tennis."

"Don't be a *fool!*" snapped her mother. "Don't be a—"

"Ladies! Ladies!" said Mr. Hammer, and this time he held up both arms like a prize-fight referee.

"Nobody's going to get suspended from anything. I'll talk to Caroline Collins myself. Nobody's going to get suspended from anything."

"Marty's been suspended from the club," said Kathy.

"Honey," said Mr. Hammer, "your Marty is a crazy lady. She's got a very, very nasty little reputation. She didn't get that for nothing."

"Well, Marty's a little direct sometimes, but . . ." Kathy faltered.

"Honey, this Marty is talking to an Italian police chief about the Mafia. She's going on with a mouth like a longshoreman. She's a crazy, crazy lady."

"She didn't do it."

"Honey. Are you aware . . . well, at a certain time of life certain women pass through a stage, particularly when they're not married and don't have kids. They get like all twisted up inside. Everything's out of proportion to them. She was a fine, fine player at one time, but she's washed up, and now, Kathy, she's gone and put all her eggs in one basket, and that basket is you."

"Listen to Mr. Hammer," said Kathy's mother.

"Honey, look. Even on the off chance she did do something of this kind, there's no way to prove it. All the cops have is a little itty bit of red clay that could have come off anybody's shoe, and that includes your mom, your sister, Oliver English, you, and even your little brother,

Bobby. Ruth herself could have gone in there for some reason. No judge would look at a case like this. Nobody is going to be arrested, Kathy. Not Marty, not anybody. The personal feud between Molina and your coach was bound to erupt over something. All we want to do is get you clear and the NELTA off our necks. Understand?"

"You're trying to pin it on Marty," said Kathy.

"Put her to bed," said Mr. Hammer without his smile.

Jody's voice suddenly rang clearly from the partially opened living-room door. "Can I come in now?" Jody asked.

"Jody, please go to bed," said her mother. "It's after ten."

"I have something to say, Mom."

"Well, say it."

"I remember when I was home alone that night. The night you're talking about. I was doing the dishes, and I put on one of my records."

"Jody, what is this about? Can it wait?" asked her father. "Mr. Hammer doesn't have much time."

"It would be helpful to Kathy."

"Come in, honey," said Mr. Hammer. "Come on in. I hear you've got a pretty strong right arm too!" He chuckled.

Jody did not smile. She sat cross-legged and composed on a hassock. "I remember exactly how I was feeling that evening," she said. "Listening to my record. I was happy to be listening to my record instead of having to listen to a baseball game on TV. I hate baseball," she added firmly to Mr. Hammer. "Anyway, I remember thinking that it was a waste because I'd looked it up in the paper that afternoon and the ball game wasn't on TV anyway."

"I don't understand," said Mr. Hammer.

"Well, it was a waste, you see, because even if I hadn't been alone in the house, I could have played my record anyway."

"Jody, you're talking in circles," said her mother. "This has nothing to do with Kathy."

"But, *Mom*, don't you see? If Kathy went to Fenway and saw a game that was *not* televised, all she has to do is give a pretty good description of it, and then she can prove she was there."

Mr. Hammer clapped his hands together. "One smart cookie you've got there!" he said. "Okay. All right. Now, come on, Kathy. We're getting somewhere. I'll have Dom D'Amico order the videotape of the game from channel six. All the games are videotaped even if they're not broadcast on TV. Any little thing you can remember, Kathy, that wouldn't be in the papers or on radio will do the trick."

It was then that Kathy realized, for the first time, that she actually might be in real trouble herself—that people might not believe her story. Suddenly she wanted to sit in her father's lap.

"Anybody go out on the field?" Mr. Hammer asked. "Any streakers, kids? Anything like that? Any fan make a spectacular catch? Anybody lean over the fence to get a foul ball? Fall on the tarp, say?"

Kathy shook her head. "Guidry was pitching," she said after a pause. "The Yanks were winning six to nothing.

Jackson hit a home run into the right-field seats."

"Something that wouldn't be in the papers, Kathy," said Mr. Hammer patiently.

"It was just . . . an old ball game. A boring one. The trouble is I was so upset about having to play Ruth the next day I could hardly concentrate. I just remember sitting there in my seat thinking I was going to be sick. Maybe default the match. Maybe I would get a migraine. I know it's awful, but I was crossing my fingers that maybe Ruth would get sick or—"

"That's a no-no, Kathy," said Mr. Hammer. "Try to remember the ball game."

"I just really remember one thing. Coming through the gate, you know? After you go up all those stairs inside the dark stadium? I remember when I saw the field for the first time. It was so green, so green . . . like an emerald with the lights on it and the sky still light. I remember how white all those little baseballs looked during the warm-up. And the Boston uniforms. So white against that green."

Mr. Hammer advised Kathy to sleep on it. He then congratulated Kathy's parents on having one daughter so talented and the other so smart. Kathy did not hear this as more than a distant buzz as she fell asleep in her chair.

8

"Where is your mind, my dear?"

Kathy did not flinch at this question. She scooped a backhand low off the court and with it hit one of the ball can targets that Marty had set up near her base line. She watched the can fall over and banged her racket head on the hard court. "I hate these courts," she said.

"It's nothing to do with the courts," said Marty. "You have played on these courts many times." She popped the ball across the net. The wind whipped unsteadily off the marina. Marty's hair flew around her head in all directions. The boats banged against one another at the dock, and Kathy realized she'd been listening more to the sounds of the boats and the crying of the gulls than to Marty. "Concentrate!" Marty ordered. Kathy knew

Marty did not like the public courts either. First because she despised anything public and also because in her playing days hard courts did not exist for anyone above the hack amateur level. Kathy became aware of a particularly large brown gull which landed on the pro-shop roof, and she netted an easy forehand.

"Are you aware, my dear, that tomorrow morning at ten o'clock you will be starting your first round in the New England Championships?"

"I know, Marty."

"Then why, please, are you looking at the quaint New England scenery that you've seen every day of your life?"

"I've hit the can twenty times, Marty. What's wrong with that?" Kathy asked. She was bent low, shifting her weight from foot to foot, holding her racket ready.

"There's nothing wrong with that. I am watching your face. There's something wrong with that, I'll tell you."

Kathy sighed loudly. "What? What's wrong with my face?"

Marty stood at the net with her hands on her hips; the gusty wind at her back still blew her hair around wildly. "A year and a half ago," she said in a bright and snappish voice, "when I first saw you play in that free clinic, I watched your expression as you hit every shot. You didn't get many balls in the court the first few times, but you hit every single one like a winner. You looked hungry and mad as a cornered cat. Also you enjoyed it. Now you look like some kind of modern dancer with her head in the clouds."

"I'm sorry, Marty. I'll concentrate. I'm cold. That's all."

"Do you think you're going to get beyond your first round tomorrow playing like a sick parakeet? You can completely destroy all the good you did yourself in Florida."

"Marty, please."

"Don't 'Marty, please' me. Get back behind that base line. Now I'm going to stand here and serve to you from the middle of the court. These are smashes, Kathy. I'm going to place the ball all over. You miss one and you get ten more. I don't care if I have to do it a hundred times. Now move your feet and you'll be cold for about two more seconds."

Gamely Kathy chased down Marty's vicious shots, which even under normal circumstances would have been difficult to return. She lunged for one and fell.

"Get up," said Marty. "Here's another one." Kathy ground her teeth together and charged across the court clumsily. When she missed it completely, Marty propped her racket against the net, folded her arms, and announced, "You are playing tennis completely without heart."

"I'm sorry, Marty."

"Do you think I've given you half your lessons free, wangled you into the Plymouth Club, and poured my lifeblood into you just to watch you fold over at your first big challenge?"

Kathy brushed at her dirty, bleeding knee and shook her head.

"What are you crying about?"

"I'm *not* crying."

"Oh! Is it raining then? Come here."

Kathy ambled up to the net. She could feel the vibrations of fury and fear in Marty more than she felt the sharp wind.

"You know, don't you?" Marty asked softly.

Kathy nodded.

"You didn't have any breakfast, I bet."

"Couldn't eat," said Kathy, wiping the cold sweat off her mouth with her sleeve.

"Come on. We'll go over to the diner. I'll get some eggs and bacon into you."

Only one other customer was present in the diner at this hour. Idly he dinted his spoon against his coffee cup as he read the paper.

"Stop that!" said Marty after he had done it for a full minute. When a plate of eggs, bacon, and English muffins was delivered to each of them, Marty announced that she had noticed Mr. Hammer's car in Kathy's driveway the evening before while she happened to be driving by. "And what did our fine, fat school superintendent have to say for himself?" she asked. Before Kathy could answer, Marty turned again to the man in the booth behind her. "If you don't stop that irritating banging," she said, "I'm going to take that spoon away from you." The man glanced at Marty with guilty eyes. He folded his paper, dropped a quarter on the table, and left.

"So!" said Marty cheerfully. "Now we're alone. Eat your eggs before they get cold. What did Mr. Hammer have to say?"

"Well, they kind of smoothed everything over," said Kathy, toying with an egg.

"Yes? And how do you like Mr. Hammer?"

"He . . . well, he scares me. I think he's a male chauvinist pig," said Kathy.

"I can do without the birdbrain lingo of your generation. What did he say?"

"Everyone seems to be . . . upset about what happened to Ruth Gumm."

"No kidding?" said Marty.

Kathy heaved a sigh. "I don't care anymore," she said.

"What don't you care about?"

"Tennis. The fun's gone out of it. I was awake all night thinking, Marty. What I was supposed to be thinking about was a ball game I went to at Fenway Park the night before Ruth drowned. If I can remember something about the game, I guess I can prove I was there. But all I could think about, over and over in my mind, was that maybe somebody who cares about me, maybe even somebody who loves me . . . did this thing for me, and if I ever have a chance to do something decent in my life, maybe I should make some sacrifice. The biggest one I could make, to kind of atone for what happened. I don't know. Maybe it isn't even a big sacrifice anymore. I don't feel like playing a game if it involves tricks like this."

"That she drowned, died, was an accident," said Marty, "no matter how you look at it."

"It doesn't matter. It was done on my behalf by somebody who . . . who . . . "

"By somebody not too nice? Is that what your Mr. Hammer, who let you cheat on an algebra exam, told you?"

"How did you know about the book he left in the room?"

"It was obvious. The minute your mother told me he was going to proctor your final exam, I put two and two together. Tell me something, my dear."

"What, Marty?"

"In all the time I've been coaching you, no matter how much of an impatient, intolerant, prejudiced old maid I may seem to be, have I ever, ever once told you to call an opponent's ball out when it's on the line? Have I ever told you to blink at a serve that just hits the back of the tape? Have I ever sat in the stands and given you a bunch of signals? Haven't I told you before every match that if you just *think* a ball is out, you call it in and give your opponent the benefit of the doubt? Haven't I?"

"Yes, Marty."

"And why do you think I've instilled this into every girl and boy I've ever coached?"

"I guess because deep down you're an honest person."

"No, my dear," Marty said, "that is not the answer at all."

Kathy sat silently, confused, as she waited for Marty to swallow her coffee. She tried to take a bite of her English muffin, but it tasted horribly dry. She washed it down with water.

"Because cheating is stupid, my dear," said Marty, glaring at Kathy's down-turned eyes. "Either you can do a thing or you can't, and that's the beginning and the end. Do you think Einstein cheated when he made up the theory of relativity? Do you think Van Cliburn cheats when he's playing at Carnegie Hall? Do you think Margaret Court ever cheated at Wimbledon? Sure you can win a few games. Maybe even up your ranking a couple of notches if you're clever, but nobody ever gets any place cheating. There will always be another Ruth Gumm around the corner for you. Do you know that?"

"Yes, Marty."

"So where the hell were you that night?"

"I told you. I went to Fenway Park."

"It sounds like you. Can't you prove it? Don't you have your ticket stub or something?"

"No, but Mr. Hammer says it doesn't matter anyway."

"Oh, it doesn't matter to the police. But it matters to the New England Lawn Tennis Association. I can tell you that. The girl's parents are raising holy hell. He can't fix them, but I can."

"What do you mean?"

"What do you think I'm doing right now?"

Kathy frowned. "Sitting having breakfast with me?"

"You are so *dense*, my dear. You're lucky you're an athlete. Of course I'm sitting here with you instead of sitting in my own office. For two whole weeks I've been turning over in my mind whether you had the gall, the stupidity, and the shallowness in your ambitious little soul to do something as pathetic and rotten as spiking that pool with chlorine. Now I'm quite convinced you didn't, and I intend to clear my own name pronto. You, my dear," she added, "wouldn't have had the brains to think of it."

In her shock and muddleheadedness Kathy ignored the insult. "You mean you've been protecting me all this time?" she asked.

"Aha!" said Marty in mock astonishment. "The fog

clears! All aircraft are now taking off and landing in Katherine Bardy's brain!"

"You think I was too *stupid*, Marty? *That's* why?"

Marty speared an enormous bite of scrambled egg, bacon, and toast with her fork, letting Kathy wait while she ate it. "No," she said at last. "Of course not, Kathy. But I do have access to your heart and soul, my dear, which even your immediate family doesn't have because they don't spend hours a day every day of the week observing you. You lost heart out there today, Kathy, because Mr. Hammer had convinced you that somebody with your future in mind might have inadvertently murdered Ruth Gumm."

Kathy winced at the word *murdered*.

"Not a nice word," said Marty, "but you can't go around saying manslaughtered. Anyway. Had you been responsible for the accident, you wouldn't have lost heart out there *today*, the morning after Hammer talked to you. You would have either lost heart the minute you heard the prank went wrong, or you wouldn't have lost heart at all. I guessed you had nothing to do with it when you played so well in Florida, but I wasn't absolutely positive until now."

"You mean you actually thought I did it?"

"Didn't you have your moments of doubt about me?" Marty asked.

"Never. Marty, I defended you like a lion in front of Mr. Hammer. I'm so glad I did, because now I know you took the rap for me."

"I'm touched, my dear. But I certainly wasn't going to take the rap, as you put it, for very long. I have my own career to think about. What I was going to do was get it out of you by hook or by crook because I know I'm the only one who could. I knew that everybody, including your slick Kenneth Hammer, was going to protect their little golden goose. If you *had* had anything to do with it, Kathy, I would have found out, and then I would have had you kicked out of the NELTA and the USTA so fast you wouldn't have known what hit you. Now I'll call up Caroline Collins, who by the way used to be a doubles partner of mine years ago when she was Caroline Shmuckler, and tell her to get the NELTA off your back." Marty signaled to the waitress. "Please take this young lady's cold breakfast away," she said, "and bring her a nice new hot one." Marty smiled. "Now, when you're finished, we'll go over to the club."

"But Marty, I thought they wouldn't let you in!" said Kathy.

"Oh, yes, they will. First of all I will clear my name immediately because I spent that entire evening, as I spend almost all evenings, at the bar of the East End Steak House, and at least ten people saw me there. Secondly, Kathy, this thing is over, and I want you to know that. It was an accident pure and simple with nobody to blame. I didn't know that until now, but of all the people at Newton that day Oliver English is much too namby-pamby to do such a thing, no matter how many cow eyes he makes at you. Your mother's too featherheaded, and Jody has a heart of twenty-four-carat gold. So as you can see, Kathy, no one did it. It's all over. A tempest in a teapot if you ask me, and I'm going to spend the entire day getting the heart back into your game."

Slowly Kathy managed to come back to herself. She slept for two hours on the beach under a towel. Later in the afternoon during a spirited rally with Marty she overheard Mr. Molina's shrill voice yelling at a beachboy for dropping a pile of chairs. "You know what I told that fat so-and-so?" Marty asked.

"What?" Kathy asked.

"Keep the head of your racket *down*, Kathy. I told him if he ever tried to make a speck of trouble for me again, he'd find his chubby rear in such hot water he'd scream like a plucked turkey. I happen to know a couple of things about Fred Molina's after-hours activities, and I told him I had a couple of Polaroid snapshots."

"But Marty, that's *blackmail!*" said Kathy, stopping and letting a ball pass by.

"Not if I don't have the photographs," said Marty. "Now go take a shower and go home and sleep."

Kathy bent at the waist and relaxed. "Thanks, Marty," she gasped.

"On second thought, it's a nice day. Do a mile in the sand."

Why don't I cheat on this? Kathy asked herself as she ran down the beach. *Why do I cheat on a math test, and then when I'm so exhausted I could drop dead, I still do a stupid mile just because* she *tells me to? She's in her office. She'll never see me.* Kathy swore at Marty every step of the way to the appointed marker at the far end of the beach, but she did not run an inch short of it all the same. *Invisible people, alive and dead,* she thought as she pedaled home slowly. *All as if they had little apartments inside my head, sitting there waiting for me to*

*make a mistake, cross them up. Then they send out a
general alarm.* She wished she could at least eliminate
Mrs. Diggins's pensive, disappointed face. "All my work.
All my hard work," was what Mrs. Diggins said when
Kathy conjured her up. In light of the algebra textbook's
having in the end proved irresistible to her Kathy knew
that should she one day earn a hundred thousand dollars
playing tennis, it would all somehow be lost to her because she couldn't count it properly. In this picture
Kathy, shabby and thin, working behind the counter of a
five-and-ten-cents store, encountered a plump, neatly
dressed Mrs. Diggins who looked on her pityingly,
clucked her tongue, and said, "Should have learned your
algebra, Katherine. Now it's too late."

The Future, as mapped out from time to time by each
of the adults in Kathy's life, always involved grave crises
that spun like globes on the pinpoints of her weaknesses.
One day her kind and handsome husband, who looked
just like Bjorn Borg, would walk out on her in despair
after she had balanced the family checkbook wrong for
the twentieth time. One day a baby might die because it
took her an hour to find a doctor's number in the phone
book or because she'd measured fractions of a formula
wrong. She had been told of these possibilities and believed them.

There was a strange car in the driveway. Kathy hesitated and went around to the kitchen door to let herself
in. As she threw her sweatbands and rackets into the
closet she was aware of an unusual silence in the living
room. When she walked into the living room, she was
greeted as if for a surprise birthday party by her mother

and father and Oliver. Was it her father's wisdom that had excluded Mr. Hammer from the house? she wondered later.

"Kathy, sit down. We have terrific news," was what her father said. He was smiling. Oliver was looking very satisfied, slouched in a hard-backed chair. The strange man sat next to her mother. "Kathy, this is Dom D'Amico . . ."

"Chief of police," underscored Kathy's mother.

"Hi, Kathy," said the chief. He was as friendly as Mr. Hammer but to Kathy less frightening, as his thighs did not bulge so in his clothing. He was a big man but wore a saggy tan suit and seemed, except for his hat, to be just a normal unscary workingman who might have come to see her father about his daughter's wedding pictures.

"Hello," said Kathy, her voice so low she could not hear it herself. "Hello," she said again after she cleared her throat.

"Kathy, your worries are over. Over!" repeated her mother.

"Let Chief D'Amico tell it," said her father. "That's what he's here for . . . please?"

"What's over?" Kathy asked.

"Kathy," the chief began. He seemed uncomfortable. "I just dropped in because your dad here and Ken Hammer said you'd believe this if it came from the horse's mouth. Well, I guess I'm the horse."

Everyone but Kathy, who was not sure what he meant, laughed at the chief's joke.

"My boys were up at the club today," he went on. "Found a cracked valve in the pool's recirculating system. Called the guy from the pool company. There was no crime, Kathy. All charges have been dropped. It was a mechanical failure, Kathy. A mechanical failure," he said again.

"What?"

"Kathy, they found a crack in the valve down in the drainage system of the swimming pool," her mother broke in. "That means—"

"In the pump," the chief went on. "The crack was near the . . . well, I won't bore you with all the technical details. But I'm here, honey, again because your dad said how important it would be for you to hear it from me. Apparently these cracks just kind of come up once in a while. One in a million. Just like an airplane. Got a crack no one can see. Everyone has all the good will in the world, but the plane comes down all the same. Same thing, Kathy. Same thing."

The chief, Kathy noticed, had the same habit as Mr. Hammer. They both used a funny shorthand way of talking.

"Anyhow," he said, "the thing was busted, and our best guess is a lot of the chlorine got backed up over a period of time, and then the whole mess went into the pool at once. Poor girl jumped into it. Anyhow. Let me make myself perfectly clear. The cause of death was drowning. There are no negligence charges. There are no other charges or investigations on the books. The slate is wiped clean, Kathy. It's over." And so was Chief D'Amico's speech as he tweaked the crown of his hat and got up to shake Kathy's father's hand.

"But what about the footprint?" Kathy asked.

Chief D'Amico paused in the doorway. "Honey," he said slowly and emphatically, "there was no crime. *No crime.* Do you understand that?"

"But . . . " Kathy began.

Chief D'Amico smiled in much the same way Mr. Hammer smiled, Kathy noticed. Patiently and kindly, as if she were a foreigner whose English was very bad. "Now listen," he said.

"*Listen*, Kathy," said her mother.

"Honey, listen," added her father.

"*I'm listening*," said Kathy.

"First of all," he said, "we don't have a footprint, honey. What we have is a little bit of red clay off a sponge. Okay? Okay. Now even if on the morning your friend drowned we had gone in there with ten detectives, I guaran-damn-tee you we would have come up with an earring here, a sneaker there, a wallet and a hot dog wrapper, and a place so full of footprints and fingerprints we'd have gone crazy. Now. Few days later the girl's parents are foaming at the mouth that someone tried to hurt their kid. Okay? Okay. We go on what we've got, Kathy. We take into consideration everything we see. And what do we see? We see a crack in a valve. We get the guy down from Medford, where they make these pools. The same guy who installed that pool years ago. He confirms it. So what do we do? We file a report saying it's our best guess that the chlorine backed up in the system and was released by accident. That this may or may not have contributed to the girl's drowning. In any case there's no crime. Now what do you want, honey? You want a Perry Mason case here? You want a lot of scandal and gossip? I hear you have a great future, by the way."

"I'm sorry," said Kathy.

"So, honey, answer me something. Okay? You tell me what evidence amounts to when there's no crime. Tell me."

"I . . . I don't understand," said Kathy.

The chief smiled in his patient way again. "Look, Kathy," he explained, "if, God forbid, I were to drop dead right here in my tracks of a heart attack, a pure, simple act-of-God heart attack, this room, this whole house is full of evidence, isn't it? You've got your dad's paper there. You've got your mom's magazine, your boy-friend's car keys, and your tennis racket, right? Okay. But there's no crime, see, because I had a heart attack. Now do you understand?"

"I think so," said Kathy. "I guess I was just confused because you said it was your *best guess* that the pump backed up. You weren't sure."

"You've got a live one here," the chief said to Kathy's mother and father. "Now look, honey. When a plane goes down, do you think they know just exactly what went wrong with it? No! If they did, there wouldn't be any more plane crashes, would there? When a plane goes down, Kathy, and two hundred people blow up, what has the FAA got? They've got a little black box with the pilot's last words, 'Roger, the wing's falling off.' "

"Kathy, Chief D'Amico is a busy man," said her mother.

"When I say our best guess, Kathy," he continued, "what I mean is our best guess. You can't run through an event of the past as if you had a movie of it. As if you had somebody there taking notes."

"Yes, sir," said Kathy. "I do understand."

"Whew!" said the chief, and once again he looked around the room as if for allies in some elaborate joke. "If she doesn't make it in tennis," he said chuckling, "she'll probably grow up to be a lady lawyer, and she'll ruin my life! If not that, then a newspaper reporter, and she'll ruin my life that way too. Only kidding, honey. I know you've had a tough week. Your mom and dad have told me all about it. You're just a youngster, and sometimes it takes awhile to let things sink in. I'm just awful sorry there was any fuss in the first place. We do our job, but you can't stop people talking. I'd give her a shot of bourbon," he said with mock slyness, "except it's illegal for me to suggest you corrupt a minor."

After many thanks and promises to buy tickets to the policemen's ball, which her parents did every year anyway, everyone said good-bye, and the chief was gone, out the screen door and into the evening light with his hat.

The first to say that Kathy didn't look really happy, or at least happy enough, was her mother.

"I don't know why, Mom," Kathy answered. "I just don't believe it."

"You mean you don't trust what he says, or you're just relieved and it hasn't sunk in? Which one?" her mother asked.

"Kathy smells a rat," said Jody, who had been sitting

in a far dark corner of the room all the while, only barely noticed by Kathy, as if she were some kind of spirit.

"For once, Jody," said Kathy's father, "there is no rat."

"According to Peachy Malone—" Jody began.

"I don't want to hear what that dingbat or any other dingbat has to say," Kathy's father interrupted.

"Peachy'd sell her mother's wedding ring for a Hershey bar," said Oliver.

"She heard exactly what the man from the pool company said," Jody went on, but her father cut her off.

"Kathy," he said, "it's been a rough week for you, but it's over. It's gone. Do you understand that?"

"I guess so, Dad," said Kathy slowly.

"What do you mean, you guess so?" Oliver put in.

"I was just thinking, no matter what the police say, somebody who went to that Newton tournament was in the pool house. Otherwise Mr. Molina wouldn't have found a footprint. That's all. And I suppose I'm a little confused because all week long, or since I *knew*, anyway, that in their hearts everyone believed I did it, or that somebody, maybe even somebody who loves me. . . I don't know, Dad. I've been thinking so hard about that game at Fenway Park. I still wish I could remember something so that forever and ever nobody would think it was me."

"But nobody *does*, Kathy," said Oliver. "You don't have to. You could go to the chief of police with a ticket stub and scorecard and your picture taken with Carlton Fisk, and he wouldn't care."

"I don't know," said Kathy. "It just seems everybody wants to hold their hands over my ears and eyes. *Every-*

thing's going to be all right. Just the way three doctors told us when Grandma had that stroke. Everything was going to be all right, but it wasn't."

Oliver announced to the general company that he thought Kathy was right. "Hiding things from her," he said, "as if she were an idiot. I'm going to fill in all the gaps," he said.

"Oliver!" warned Kathy's mother.

"What harm is it going to do now, Mrs. B.?" he asked.

Kathy's mother stood and went into the kitchen. "All right," she said. "Have it your way. Somebody's got to do the cooking around here," she added. "Somebody's got to make supper."

Oliver knelt on the floor directly in front of Kathy so that she looked down at his face. He took both her hands in his. Kathy was struck at how bony his knees seemed in his oversized chinos. His lock of unruly black hair fell over his eyes as usual and caught just under his large tortoiseshell glasses. "Let me tell you everything, Kathy," he said. "Nobody wanted to tell you before because we thought it would make you upset."

"And you might lose a tennis game," Jody piped up from the corner.

"Shut up, Jody," said Oliver wrathfully. "You're the one who has the big mouth around here. You promised to shut it, and all you accomplished with your gossip and your Peachy Malone was to upset Kathy all over again. Didn't you?" He wouldn't let Jody's opened mouth say a word. "Okay, Kathy, every single one of us was talked to by the cops. Did you know that?"

Kathy shook her head. "You?" she said.

"Yup. Very easy. No trips in the squad car to the station house. No fingerprinting, no mug shots . . ." Oliver was smiling, then he seemed to realize perhaps he shouldn't be. Kathy had faced enough big smiles. "Me and Jody and your mom as well as Marty. They asked me a few questions while I was lifeguarding at the club. They came to the house while you weren't here to talk to your mom and dad and Jody. Apparently they found out I put those tacks under my mom's husband's tires six years ago. They even knew about Jody hitting the nurse."

"They did?"

"Yes, they did. But it was all very easy, Kathy. Even if somebody had gone down to where the chlorine was kept, they'd have had to do it in the dark while the cocktail party was going on. The pool was closed that night, they turned the lights off and closed the gate. I watched Molina lock up at nine. He vouched for me, by the way. He never lets his staff serve drinks without a shoeshine inspection first. Sure enough, he remembered that I was wearing my black cordovans. The druggist in Norwood said that yes, your mom had been there, and unless she flew, that's an hour's drive one way, so she was off the hook. Of course your dad was with Bobby at the clinic, and he didn't even go to the Newton tournament anyway. The druggist was helpful. He remembered calling this house wondering if your mom had left. He got Jody, naturally, and Mrs. Diggins had called earlier, so there you are. Now you can't find any holes in that, Kathy, so don't you go worrying about people who love you. This is proven stuff, Kathy. It's been checked out."

Except for me. I haven't been checked out, Kathy thought, but she didn't say so. Uncertainty must have still been in her eyes though, because Oliver looked at her sadly as if he hadn't said enough, or hadn't said it right.

When the speculation over the dinner table became unbearable to Kathy, because she didn't think she would be the New England fourteen-and-under champion within the next eight days, she pushed back her chair and announced she was going out.

"I didn't do my mile in the sand today," she lied. "Have to keep my legs in shape."

"Your legs are in shape, Kathy," said her mother. "It's going to get dark. Not right after you've eaten . . ."

"Marry Kathy," said Jody to Oliver, "and you'll have a lifetime of dishes to do. She'll go jogging in ten feet of snow to get out of it."

As usual Jody had the last word, and as usual Kathy ran to the Redmonds' house.

As she jogged, slowly because she was still tired, she looked at the shadows from the trees on the houses and the lawns. There was a darkness in the still-bright sunshine. The houses on Ocean Drive seemed bigger and more imposing than usual. Julia's mother, Kathy recalled, was always complaining about the cost of maintaining a house near the sea. The brass needed polishing every day because of the salt in the air. The spruce shrubs around the front of the house turned brown and died on the oceanward side and had to be replaced every year. The best paint peeled off the house quickly, and the grass grew crabbed in the sandy soil. One by one as she passed them by Kathy stared at the houses of the rich. Squirreled away in those many high-ceilinged bedrooms, dressing rooms, and sewing rooms were the two possessions belonging only to the people with very real money: servants and ghosts. Still Kathy did not think there was a better place on earth than Massachusetts on the sea, with the late summer's light grown ripe like a peach on a windowsill.

In the Redmonds' living room the light was gold. The gold word *Steinway* on the baby grand was readable from across the room, and the cherrywood bookcases and paneling appeared to have a vast depth beneath their polish, as if a person could poke a finger deep into the wood itself. Julia lay stretched out flat in the middle of the living-room rug.

"Katherine," said Julia's mother, "I know you have something on your mind, but I'm not letting you stay up late with this night owl here. Your mother has called, and I made her a solemn promise. You," she said in Julia's direction, "are going to have to start rising before eleven. Lazy young thing! School begins in a couple of weeks. At nine o'clock, Kathy, I am driving you home. You are not trotting home. . . ."

"Jogging, Mother," Julia corrected.

"You are not trotting home. I am going to drive you. Now don't you girls eat up all the ice cream." Mrs. Redmond let herself out of the living room carrying an armful of gladiolas. Once she looked back with amusement in her eye, as if she thought there was a real chance that her daughter and Kathy might be running a secret numbers racket.

For a long moment both girls were silent, Julia still stretched full out on the sun-warmed rug and Kathy sitting with her legs pulled up under her chin, distractedly biting one knee. At the other end of the hall, at the curved end of the dining room, were four stained-glass windows which Julia always called "stain glassed." In that room, when they were about seven, Kathy and Julia had played a game called Pope and Nun, not because either of them was particularly religious but because of the pious invectives of Rose, who took both *The Irish Echo* and *The Catholic News* and read from them aloud over tea. Happily Julia and Kathy, dressed in red velvet curtains, had excommunicated each other in the blue, red, and yellow light of those windows.

"What is it, kiddo?" Julia asked.

Haltingly and disjointedly Kathy told her about Mr. Hammer and the algebra exam, about Jody and Peachy Malone and the chlorine and the red clay, about Marty and Chief D'Amico and how it felt to know everybody was trying to make things all right, to make things disappear, and then when they had disappeared, all those things, how that felt too. "It makes me think of my grandma," Kathy explained. "You remember when she broke her hip, how it all healed up after a while, but she was still afraid to walk? Afraid to use that broken bone even if there was nothing wrong with it and it was stronger than before because of the steel pin? That's sort of the way it is. I have a big tournament starting tomorrow morning, and it's as if I'm afraid to . . . to play."

"Oh, Kathy," said Julia, groaning and rolling onto her stomach.

"I know there's nothing much you can do. I just wanted to come over and tell you."

Julia's index finger traced a floral pattern in the rug beneath her. "You know I had a nightmare once," she said. "There was a terrible thunderstorm in the middle of the night. This summer. The noise of it went right into my dream. I was sure the atomic bomb had been dropped. I woke up and I ran to the window to see the mushroom cloud over Boston. I was sure it was the end of the world, but it was just a crack of thunder. I remember standing at my window. Mom came in to close my window, but I wouldn't let her. I just let the rain blow in on me and soak me because I was so glad there was no bomb. I think you've got to look at it that way, Kathy. Do you know what I mean?"

"I know," said Kathy.

"Well, what's worrying you exactly?"

"Well, one thing is Jody told me—just before dinner tonight when I went upstairs to wash my hands and change—Jody told me Peachy was listening the whole time the guy from the pool company was talking to the cops today. There was an argument because the guy from the company said that the valve had cracked when the pool was drained suddenly. He said the pool had to be drained over a long period the way they usually do at the end of the summer. Otherwise there's too much pressure and something gives. But the cops said it couldn't be proven either way, so they dropped the whole thing. The thing of it is, I know old Fred Molina. He'd never let a crack go unrepaired. He's like a German soldier about everything."

"Kathy, even Fred Molina is human. He can make a mistake."

"Maybe," said Kathy, wondering suddenly what Marty had meant by his "after-hours activities."

"I do notice, by the way, that it's Jody who's been the one to upset you both times in this whole business."

"God, everybody, even you, Julia, everybody's talking about my getting upset as if I were a white rat with some rare disease."

"Well, Jeez Louise, Kathy. What do you want me to say?"

"I'm sorry. Go on."

"Well, I do think it's Jody's fault. She's so very jealous of you."

"Jody's just . . . very moral."

Julia made an impolite noise at this and snorted, "Moral shmoral. Look at Peachy Malone, who's been gossiping with her. Peachy's about as reliable as Rose. Jody's a nice kid, Kathy, but she's jealous of you, and she also always, *always* has to get her two cents in. She'd make a great jury member. She's the type who'd dead-lock the whole thing for three weeks in the motel until everybody else goes stark raving nuts. I'll tell you one thing. People like this pool company guy are liars. Just like the electric company creeps at the nuclear plant. They're forever saying nothing's their fault."

"I didn't think of it that way," Kathy admitted.

"The thing is over, Kathy. Put it out of your mind."

"I would if I could do one thing."

"What's that?"

"If I could think of one single happening that would prove to everybody that I was out at Fenway Park that night, then it would be over for me. Unless I do, I feel sort of as if I have a terrible mark against me. Look how they went after Marty and Oliver and Mom and even Jody, who, by the way, was decent enough to cover for me. Asking them police questions. Did they do it to me? No. Because I'm the precious little golden talent. I hate the word *talent*."

"First of all that's completely untrue. You were in Florida when this whole thing came to light. By the time you got home, the thing had blown over. It has nothing to do with precious golden talent, which, by the way, you happen to have."

Kathy still gnawed at her knee. "Talent," she said. "People who can draw and write and play music have talent."

"What's wrong with playing tennis?"

"Nothing's wrong with it. It just requires . . . it takes everything out of me. Everything, after a match. Before a match."

"So does giving a concert."

"Yes, and I can't get up on the stage, Julia. I just think in the back of everybody's mind is going to be a little question. Did she do it or didn't she? I was even considering giving the whole thing up and never playing tennis again."

Julia got up slowly and went over to a window seat. The sun had set, and the light was dying on the grass outside. Julia had always been too fastidious to swear.

Kathy was numbed by the string of words she heard Julia whisper.

"Julia!" she began, but Julia cut her off.

"Look, Kathy," she said. "You have to look at this thing a whole new way. You have to imagine something here. Then nothing that anyone thinks will be important anymore. Please try and imagine one thing."

Kathy bit her knee hard. "What?" she asked.

"If you had done it, kiddo, you'd know it, wouldn't you?"

"I guess so."

"Even if nobody else in the world knew, you'd know it. Even if Mr. Molina had never come up with his sponge full of red clay, or if Ruth's parents had never made a fuss, you'd still know it, wouldn't you, and you'd have to live with it for the rest of your life."

"I . . . I guess I would."

"It would sit there inside you, like some incurable ulcer, like a big bleeding, weeping boil in the middle of your stomach for the rest of your days, but you don't have to live with it, Kathy, because you didn't do it!"

Kathy felt her spine sag after a stunned second or two. "You know," she said, "everyone else has said what sounds right, the right thing to say, but you're the only one who's said what *is* right. I never thought of that. I wish . . ."

After a long silence Julia asked, "What?"

"I don't know. I wish I could say how much I thank you."

"Yankee!" said Julia from the darkness across the room. There was a great sadness in her voice that Kathy could not place.

9

Rain had been predicted for southern New England, but the day broke clear and bright as crystal over Newport, Rhode Island.

Kathy's mother read aloud from her notes on the yellow lined pad. "A nice girl," she said, "so forth and so on. She was Rhode Island champion in twelve and under. Very consistent serve but not too powerful. No nerves. Remember that. Now—"

"Look!" Kathy interrupted, standing dead still in the long dark archway that led to the courts. Framed perfectly by the blackened bricks was the brilliant grass in the morning sun. Kathy drew a sudden sharp breath and felt her eyes widen. *So like my first look at the field in Fenway Park*, she thought.

"What?" asked her mother.

"It's so *green*, Mother."

"She's fast," Kathy's mother continued, "laterally, but she's apparently slow coming up to the net. Hesitates. Kathy, are you going to stand there and let everyone bump into you? Come on. Let's find Susie Chan, and you two can hit together before your matches. Before you do, just let me finish here. There's Daddy and Jody. Do they see us? Okay. Now just let me finish."

Crowds of players streamed by, but Kathy's eyes were fixed on the courts ahead of her. They were a near jungle green. "Come on, Mom. I'll beat Mary Strolle. You don't have to go through all that."

"Will you look at me while I'm talking to you?" her mother asked. "This isn't Mary Strolle. This is your first round, Kathy. Bourke . . . no, Bourne. It took me hours to assemble these notes. You could at least listen. Now remember—" Kathy's mother flipped a page over. "Okay. Not one single service fault in her last three tournaments. Look for that serve to go in, and she'll move it around too. Kathy, are you listening? What are you looking at?"

"The grass, Mom," Kathy answered. She set her rackets and bag down at the side of an unused court. Then she took off her sneakers and began to pad around on it in her bare feet.

"Will you please get that foolish grin off your face, Kathy, and put your shoes on? What is everybody going to think? You've seen grass before."

"Not like this," said Kathy, and she reluctantly withdrew from the court.

"There's Susie. Now I'm going to find Daddy."

"Okay, Mom," Kathy said, her eyes following the languid and perfectly schooled play of a girl on the neighboring court. It was a clay practice court. Probably the girl didn't mind because she was used to grass. Probably she was a member here and had been all her life, Kathy thought, taking note of her expensive clothes, her perfect complexion, and the way the girl tossed her head to clear her face of a shiny blond page boy. Certain members of the Plymouth Bath and Tennis Club had belonged all their lives, had been children there and now brought their own children to the same courts and the same pool and the same beach. This girl, Kathy calculated, was of that type. She would one day bring four children as perfectly blond, clean, and well tailored as herself to this club, and she would sit and sip a tall drink with a piece of mint in it from the flower-filled café that stood at the entrance to the clubhouse.

Kathy and Susie Chan found a grass court in fair condition. Before they began to practice, they both walked back and forth over it several times, giggling.

"Who's your first round?" Kathy asked.

Susie groaned. "Jenny Robbins," she answered.

"Oh, poor you. Bad luck."

"My only hope," said Susie, returning a forehand to Kathy, "is that she's as bad as I am on this stuff. It's like playing on a sponge!"

"Better get used to it, Susie," Kathy said, grinning. "Wimbledon's all grass!"

"That's for you, Kathy," said Susie Chan cheerfully. "I'll never see England except from a tourist bus."

"Come on," said Kathy.

"You know what people are saying about you, Kathy, since that tournament down in Florida?"

"Come on," Kathy repeated.

"No, I mean it," Susie declared seriously. She stopped their rally and came up to the net. "I'd almost rather draw Jenny Robbins than you, Kathy. Jenny's a terrific player, but she's not going to improve. You're on your way, Kathy. Everybody knows it. By the end of the week you should be the New England fourteen and under champion." Susie stepped back and chopped a ball over the net. She smiled confidently. "You know what the *Globe* said about you, Kathy. 'How's the fierce young ball of fire who looks like a junior Rosie Casals?' "

"Oh, garbage," said Kathy.

"It's not garbage," Susie answered, reaching for an overhead that eluded her completely. "Now will you look at that? I kicked up a divot. Do you think they'll make me pay for it?"

Kathy waited for Susie Chan to replace the small mound of grass and earth. She leaned over and ran her knuckles over the tender green blades, not daring to lie down and put her cheek against them, although she would have loved to. *This is where you belong*, she told herself, hoping to stop the fluttering in her stomach. *You've earned it and you deserve it and there will be more grass courts someday. Just like there were for Marty. This is where you belong. Do you?* said another voice in her head. She wondered if Susie Chan, so happy and free of cares, had heard much about Ruth. People talked. Did Susie know? Were there people out there who were saying, "Oh, they just covered the whole thing up. They just kept everything quiet." *Stop it, Kathy*. The good sensible voice was back again. *It's over. Nobody did anything to anybody. Nobody thinks anything about you except that you're a great player*. This voice was worth listening to because it was Jody's. Even Jody was convinced and had told her so last night when she'd come home from Julia's house. As she and Susie resumed their rally Kathy hoped Susie would remember how she'd tried to be helpful with the dreadful poison ivy medicine rather than think she was the kind of person who would . . . she couldn't use the word.

"How do you like the grass?" Jody's real live voice piped up from behind the court. The change in Jody since the evening before could not have been more stunning had she claimed to have found a true religion.

"Spongy," said Kathy, "but . . . nice!" She smiled at Jody between shots. When Jody made up her mind about something, there was no turning her around. The year before, Kathy guessed, Jody had made up her mind to hate tennis, to hate the endless weekends of tournaments, to hate the tennis talk at the supper table. Kathy had figured this would be a fact of life as long as she lived with her family. Quite unaccountably Jody alone had waited up for her the night before. Jody never waited up or seemed glad to see her, at least not since they had been children. "I'm sorry, Kathy," Jody had announced strongly and with no reluctance the moment Kathy walked in the front door. Kathy had simply stared at her, curled on the sofa in the lamplight.

"What? Sorry for what?" she'd asked.

"I'm sorry I passed on that stupid gossip of Peachy's

about the pool man," Jody said. "It was wrong of me to do that. Peachy was probably just trying to bribe more ice cream out of me. Another thing, Kathy."

"What?" Kathy had asked, astonished.

"I really do want you to win the New England championship."

"Really, really, really?" asked Kathy, joking because she did not yet believe Jody.

"Really," Jody went on solemnly. "I didn't know you had it in you, Kathy, to consider giving up tennis because of what happened to Ruth. I thought you were too hard and too desperate."

There had been no appropriate answer in Kathy's mind to this statement. She had just taken off her jacket, folded it, and sat on the floor, staring wordlessly up at her sister.

"I always thought," Jody added, "that you would do anything to win a tennis match. I was wrong."

"You mean . . ." Kathy stumbled over her thoughts. "You mean somewhere along the line you thought maybe I'd done it? Put the chlorine in the pool?"

"Never," Jody answered stoutly. "But I didn't know you had it in you to give up tennis if somebody else did it on your behalf. That's real honor, Kathy, real honor." Jody stressed the word as if she were lecturing on the difference between diamonds and zircons. "It made me think too. Maybe we all got something out of that terrible accident after all. You showed your true colors as an unshallow person, and now I've decided not to be jealous anymore. Ever again."

Every cloud has a silver lining, Kathy had thought

when Jody had announced her intention. *Maybe*, added that faraway other voice in the back of her mind.

As it always happened, things looked brighter in the bright sun. Jody sat cross-legged at the edge of the court, dutifully reading a book about playing tennis on various surfaces. From time to time she read aloud bits of wisdom about untrue bounces, running without slipping, and dry yellow patches.

Miss Bourne, or was it Bourke? Kathy was not sure of her first or last name. Nonetheless she had a very good passing shot. *All I have to do to beat her*, Kathy instructed herself, *is play my best and concentrate*. The match was beginning to take too long. Kathy knew that. Her concentration was not at its best. Kathy had taken one look at her opponent, and instead of thinking about the girl's strokes, she thought about her shining, straight hair, which Kathy envied, and her tall, well filled out figure, which Kathy also envied, and just the air about her, which suggested a very large room with a pink-canopied bed matching a pink fluffy rug. Win or lose, this girl would go home happy tonight because, Kathy figured, a John Travolta-like boyfriend would be waiting for her in a sparkling convertible sports car and her mother wouldn't mind.

"Idiot!" Kathy yelled at herself. Silently she bullied herself. *This girl shouldn't take you to three sets. You should have finished her off by now, six-four, six-two. You had her down two service breaks, and now she's even again. Idiot. One more lousy error and you're going to lose your serve.*

The girl had what Marty would call a nice old-fashioned lady's game. She could run like a deer back and forth on the base line, always ready for whatever Kathy gave her. Kathy served hard. For one agonizing moment the ball tipped on the tape of the net and then fell back on her own side. Double fault. Now Miss Bourne, or Miss Bourke, was ahead a break. *Where is your mind, my dear?* Kathy asked herself, but not aloud. Something had triggered an irritation in the back of her thinking. It was as annoying and persistent as the neighbors' television set late at night when she was trying to fall asleep. She couldn't see it, and she couldn't really hear the words, but it hummed there all the same.

"Stupid, dumb idiot. Give up the game, you turkey!" she yelled when a smash went out. "What did you do *that* for? You had the whole court to hit. You could have dinked it over the net. She was way out of position. Instead you have to try and hit the line. Idiot!" Kathy threw her racket against the net.

"Kathy Bardy," came the umpire's warning.

"I'm sorry," said Kathy immediately.

She sat for her allotted minute during the changeover and tried to breathe and to concentrate. *Mental garage sale!* she told herself. *Everything goes! Everything goes out of your mind except this match. This next game. If you lose the next game, you're out of the tournament in the first round. Now get out there and serve four aces. Have I lost heart after all?* she wondered, panicking suddenly. *Is this what it's like to play without heart? Win a few and lose a few?*

Kathy caught Jody's eye. Jody was watching intently,

not reading, from a folding chair behind the court. *And she's pulling for me*, Kathy thought. *Look at her face. Oh, how they're all pulling for me.* Her mother's face and her father's were puzzled and strained. Even little Bobby was quiet. He rubbed his bare feet back and forth over the grass, hanging suspended between Jody's knees.

Kathy stood ready to serve. She waited for a stray ball from the neighboring court to be retrieved. She bent to bounce her own ball twice before she served. Then she remembered. The white tennis ball against the green grass.

"Thirty seconds," said the umpire's dry voice. "Serve please, Kathy."

"What?" Kathy heard herself ask.

"Kathy Bardy," said the umpire, "this is your last warning. Delaying play of the game results in a penalty of one game. Miss Bourne will win the match if I penalize you."

"I'm sorry," said Kathy. "I didn't realize . . . I didn't mean to." She began to laugh. She served an ace, and then another, and from that moment Miss Bourne did not win another point.

After the match Kathy apologized to the umpire and Miss Bourne. "I think I'm allergic to the grass," was all she could manage to say.

"So long as you're not allergic to good court manners," the umpire had answered huffily. But Kathy didn't care. She was too happy.

She won her second round that afternoon in twelve games.

When the day was over and she sat in the backseat of

the car with Jody and Bobby, she shared only the fact that she was pleased to have won. She wondered if she would have, had it not been for the girl three courts down the line who took off a shoe and emptied a pebble out of it. At first the memory had seemed distant and trivial. She had forced it back and back, trying only to think of the game at hand, but the white ball against the green had done it, and the picture, as clear as a photograph, popped out of its own accord, and all because someone shook a tiny bit of stone out of a shoe in exactly the same way that the Red Sox first baseman had done weeks before when she'd gone to Fenway Park. Carl Yastrzemski had sat down on first base, removed his left shoe, shaken out a bit of something, and retied it. He'd stood up and gotten a clap on the back from the Yankee coach. This had happened directly after the national anthem was over, at just the time when the camera panned the infield, player by player, starting at first base.

What a dope they'd think I was if I told them, Kathy decided, and she kept this and the private war she'd been having with herself inside. She had to do one more thing. Then it would indeed be over forever.

"Let her go," said Kathy's father. "Let her go. She just wants to run over and tell Marty, I bet. Maybe Julia." Kathy had jumped out of the car the moment they had pulled into the driveway. She left her rackets on the seat, grabbed her bicycle, and raced off down the street. Yes, she would tell Marty and especially Julia, but not just yet.

Did thunderclouds ever vanish, Kathy wondered, and leave those silver linings people talked about up there in the sky? She pictured a cloud's silver lining as a sprightly blue-gray silk, just like the lining of her mother's spring coat but in the classic puffy shape of a cumulus cloud. For the first time since Ruth had died, Kathy felt able to breathe to the very bottom of her lungs. She was able to smile, not for someone else but all alone, riding a bicycle down the street, and she could not recall having done that in several weeks. The dwarf dream would go now. *Of course they'll all think I'm silly, beating a dead horse,* she told herself, but Kathy wouldn't have given up the pebble in the unknown girl's shoe for a hundred silver trophies.

Completely out of breath, she abandoned her bicycle sloppily against the granite wall of the Plymouth police station. She yanked open the heavy glass doors and stood, panting, at what appeared to be the main desk.

The officer behind the desk looked up, opened his mouth, and blinked. "You'll have to wait a minute," he said after sizing up Kathy's wildly blown hair and impatient hands. Then he continued asking questions of a wispy little man, no bigger than a jockey, with a badly cut lip, who stood shaking between two very large policemen. "Name, please?" he asked calmly of Kathy when the wispy man had at last been hauled down a corridor.

"Kathy—Katherine Bardy. I have to see Chief D'Amico right away," Kathy answered in a rush.

"Complaint?"

"I don't have any complaints," said Kathy. "I mean I just have to see him. It's a matter of life and death," she added, trying to sound grave and smoothing down her hair with both hands.

"Honey, the chief is a busy man," the officer began.

"Oh, please, sir. Please just tell him I'm here. I know he'll say it's okay. I won't take up much of his time."

"Well, it's been a slow day," the officer allowed. "Please fill in your name, address, place and date of birth here." He handed Kathy a paper and sighed, and then he repeated Kathy's name into a telephone. "You should've told me," he said to Kathy when he'd hung up. "I didn't recognize you. Plymouth's major league star! How about that! Go right in, honey. Down the hall, up the stairs to your right. First office at the head of the stairs. Congratulations," he added when Kathy was halfway down the hall. She heard him say something about having voted for Bobby Riggs.

Chief Dom D'Amico suppressed a yawn and managed to turn it into a broad smile when Kathy walked in. "Isn't every day I get a pretty young thing coming down these halls," he said.

Kathy patted her hair again. She was dripping wet from her bicycle ride.

"Nice break from some of these no-goods and junkies and half-dead battered wives with beer on their breath. What can I do for you, honey? How did you do today, by the way?"

"Pretty well," said Kathy, trying to sound very modest. "I guess I won and all, but it's just the first two rounds. Tomorrow will be tough."

"Hear you're a sure shot to win the whole thing. Sort of like the World Series of kids' tennis?"

"Well, almost," said Kathy. "Chief D'Amico, may I ask you a favor?"

"Sure, honey. Anything my weary bones can deliver," he said, wiping his mouth on his bare arm.

Kathy cleared her throat and straightened her tennis dress. She felt desperately stupid and wished she'd gone over what she had meant to say. "I know you're going to think I'm awfully stupid," she began.

"Not a bit, honey. What's on your mind?"

"Well, could you imagine how you'd feel, Chief D'Amico, if you thought you had some kind of a terrible mark against you and that people thought bad things about you, and you wanted to clear the air once and for all?"

"Honey, I've got more black marks against me than the ten of spades, but I think I know what you're getting at."

"Well, it's just this way, sir. Mr. Hammer . . . Mr. Kenneth Hammer told me you'd ordered a videotape of the ball game the night before Ruth drowned. He said channel six has videotapes of all the games. This one wasn't broadcast."

Chief D'Amico smiled patiently, or was it impatiently? Kathy was not sure.

"Anyway," she went on, "it's just been bothering me so much. This whole thing. You see, I went to Fenway Park that night, Chief D'Amico. I didn't save my stub or my scorecard. But today in the middle of my first match I remembered something crucial. Something nobody could fake if they hadn't been to the ball game and actually seen it, and I know it would be on the tape because they always run the camera over the infield players in the same order every game. It was right after the national anthem was over. Carl Yastrzemski was playing first. He had something bothering him in his shoe. He sat right down on top of the first-base bag and took the shoe off. It was his left shoe. He emptied out a small white stone. Then he got up, and the Yankee first-base coach patted him on his left shoulder with his right hand. Then the coach folded his arms just like this and spat into the dirt on his left side. The coach was wearing a jacket even though it was a hot night. I remember that because no other player or coach wore their jacket, and I wondered how he could stand it or if he had a cold. Please, Chief D'Amico. If you could run that tape for me, you could see it for yourself. And if you would tell Ruth's mother and father and also Mrs. Collins at the New England Lawn Tennis Association who called you, I would be so grateful. I would feel one hundred percent free at last." Kathy gasped after she had said this.

The chief sat behind his desk, leaning on his elbows and playing all the while with a stubby pencil. He gave Kathy a part laughing and part frowning expression, and then he raised both hands as if in despair over a crossword puzzle. "Honey, honey, honey," he began.

"Oh, please, sir. It would mean everything to me for the rest of my life."

"I know. I can see that. Just listen a minute, okay?"

"Yes, sir," Kathy answered.

"First of all," he began, out of the side of his mouth as he lit a cigarette, "to begin with, honey, I saw you were real upset last night. Wanna make an apology that I probably went a little quick for you. Didn't realize how keyed up you were. I had a tough day. You know? I wish there were more kids like you in this world, honey. That kind of came to me when I was driving home last night. They give you a snort of whiskey, by the way?"

"Oh, no," Kathy answered. "I'd get sick if I just smelled that stuff."

"Huh," said the chief, grinning again and closing an eye against the smoke. "Just what I mean. I wish there were more kids like you. I get teen-age alcoholics down here I could tell you about . . . I got two young kids myself. I hope someday, if either one of 'em gets in a jam, he has the honesty to behave like you. Tough. Won't take half an answer." He waited, one eye still closed.

"Thank you, Chief D'Amico," said Kathy. "Now may we look at the tape?"

"Hold your horses, Kathy. The tape was sent back. But as I said, I admire your spunk. I guess that's an old-fashioned word. I mean to say your spirit and your good conscience, Kathy. Now, if you like, I'll go and call Channel Six and get the tape back, and we can sit here and watch Carl Yastrzemski take off his shoes and spit in the dirt, but I guarantee you it's unnecessary. The girl's parents are satisfied, Kathy, and so is your Mrs. Collins. I saw to that myself because I kind of thought you'd like me to. Everything is cleared up. We did a lab test on the clay, and nobody who went near the Newton Country Club had any connection with the pool house that day or any other day unless they wore gloves and walked on their hands."

"I don't understand," said Kathy. "Lab test?"

"Honey—this fella, Molina?"

"Yes?"

"Okay. We got this fella Molina yelling it isn't his fault. Right? He's yelling about people, particularly this tennis coach, tracking up his pool house with tennis court clay. He shows us a sample, and sure enough, it's red clay all right. Anybody could see that. Now what happens is this. Any time the police department investigates something, we do a routine lab test on whatever we pick up. I hardly bothered to look at the lab report, Kathy, because there was never a *real* case here. No pranks, no murders!" He arched his eyebrows over this word as if it were slightly smutty.

"You mean it was all a big hoax or something about the clay? Are you sure?"

"Kathy, do you know anything about investigations? About the D.A.'s work? About inquests?"

"No, I guess not."

"Your ideas about crime—now I'm not making fun here, Kathy, this goes for ninety-nine percent of the adult population. Most people's ideas are straight out of *Hawaii Five-O* or what's her name, the detective writer. Do you understand even if we had a bloody hand print here, the D.A. would never go near this with a ten-foot pole? If the state chose to prosecute every last two-bit accident case as a homicide, we'd be booked up into the next century. In this instance there wouldn't have even been a preliminary inquest, Kathy, because you've got too many people running around the area dropping bathing caps and sunglasses all day long. Number two, you've got a motive about as farfetched as my Aunt Ethel taking a potshot at the President. Number three, you've got your mechanical failure. Any one of those things would be enough to get a judge to laugh it out of court in two minutes. Now, if you still want me to get those tapes, I will, because you're a decent, honest kid, and I don't want to see you running around feeling like a heel inside."

"Well . . . I guess not," said Kathy. "I'm so happy, though. And you told Ruth's mother and father? You really did? And you told Mrs. Collins?"

"Called them the minute the guy from the pool company came down, Kathy. The parents were real nice, by the way. My guess is they felt a little ashamed to have made such a fuss about it. Volunteered themselves to call your Mrs. Collins. So here's a Xerox of the analysis if you want a souvenir."

Kathy shook Chief D'Amico's outstretched hand. "I'm so sorry to have bothered you," she said. "But what does this mean?" she asked, pointing out a sentence on the report.

Chief D'Amico appeared to be bored, like a doctor with a very healthy but inquisitive patient. "Huh?" he asked, his hands in his pockets. "Oh, that? That's your chemical formula for tennis court clay. See, it's completely different from our sample. Our sample is some kind of sculptor's clay. Right here."

"Sculptor's clay?"

"Yup. See. Called Plastilina. Imported from France. Comes in great big sacks—mixed or in powder form. Cheaper in powder form apparently. No mistaking it. Now you go get a good night's sleep and go win it for old

Plymouth. I'll see if I can get your name inscribed on the Rock. Okay, champ?"

Kathy was not sure whether it was a long while or a very short while in which she stood astride her bicycle, gazing at a piece of a candy bar that was stuck in the gutter. People seemed inclined to bump into her and to stare at her. She did not know where to go. *If only*, she kept repeating to herself. *If only. If only I hadn't been so pigheaded as to pursue this down to the last stupid detail, then I wouldn't know. If only Julia had not come over with Miss Greco's head the night before Ruth died. If only I hadn't gone running and seen Miss Greco's footsteps covered with red clay dust. If only I'd gone in another direction. If only a hundred things.*

"Miss, are you all right?" a woman asked.

"Yes, fine," said Kathy automatically. The people on the street bobbed up and down before her dreamily. Kathy pulled her bicycle off the sidewalk and began to pedal it away in the first direction that occurred to her. She found herself heading toward the club and the sea.

Where are the very beginnings of things? she asked herself, hoping to find some relief in what logical processes she could manage. *Where did this thing have a root? Was it because I, at least in Julia's eyes, saved Julia's life three years ago by dragging her and carrying her a mile when she fell out of that pine tree? Was it because I saved Julia's dignity on the second day of school?* Kathy thought not. *Was it because she, Kathy, had "no protective coloring," as Julia had put it, and because she needed so terribly much from Julia and Julia had chosen to freely give?*

If only, Kathy began again, *if only I hadn't bothered to go down to the police station, then at least I wouldn't know. I don't want to know. Why wasn't it enough for me to just know that I didn't do it?* She tried to picture life without tennis.

There would be school, of course, and friends and boys and movies and parties, she supposed. Jody's life had no tennis or anything as consuming as tennis in it. Jody was happy. She, Kathy, had been sublimely content before it had occurred to her to pick up a tennis racket. *I can always go back to that*, she told herself. *You can never go back*, said a quick voice in the back of her mind. *Ruth is dead, in part because of you. As much as Julia never meant in her wildest dreams to end Ruth's life, Julia has to live with what happened, and as much as your connection to it is as thin as a spider's thread, it is part of your life too now.*

The parking lot of the Plymouth Bath and Tennis Club was empty. Kathy dropped her bicycle on the stones. Although it was still August, the afternoon was cool. Seeing it was low tide, Kathy made her way slowly down the slippery jetty to her hiding place behind the pointed rock.

The pools of water that had collected there were not warm from the sun, and the seaweed in them was not spring green but nearly black. Kathy stood and peered over the top of the sheltering pointed rock. There was no one there but her. The pool and the clubhouse were closed for the day. The tennis courts were gated and locked. No human soul was around for all the distance she could see.

She cleared her throat self-consciously, although she alone was there to laugh at herself. "God?" Kathy asked of the steely gray waves. "Shall I quit tennis? Do you want me to give it up? Because I will if you want me to—I'll come back with every racket I own and throw them in the sea!"

God did not answer.

Julia did: "If you had done it, Kathy, you would have to live with it for the rest of your life. Like a big bleeding, weeping boil in the middle of your stomach for the rest of your days," said Julia, "but you don't."

Rain was expected in southern New England. It began to fall in the distance, against the bright southern sky. It poured down over the Vineyard and the Cape like a great navy sheet, over the emerald green grass at Newport. Soon it would veer north and fall on Plymouth, on Kathy's front yard, on Julia's house, and in the swimming pool where Ruth had once been alive.

From the most passionate and sensual depths of her guts Kathy howled, "Julia!" to the newly sprung east wind, but Julia was not there. Giving her up would be infinitely trickier than throwing a racket into the sea.